Dying to Live Again

A Rapper's Tale of Revelation, Redemption, and Revolution

by

Christopher E. Johnson

Dedication

This book is dedicated to the loving memory of my sister Gloria.

Acknowledgements

I thank my family members for their support in the creation of this literary work.

I thank my pastor, Pastor Terrell Monger, for encouraging me to follow my dreams.

TABLE OF CONTENTS:

Chapter 1:

Dead Man Talking

Familiar old-school thumping bass permeates my silver minivan as I drive across the San Rafael Bridge in the direction of San Quentin State Prison. The irony is not lost on me that the same man spitting rhymes through my speakers is the very same man I'm on the way to visit, a beefed-up *brotha* sitting deep inside the bowels of the segregated section of death row in the so-called "North Block" section where the most well behaved of the condemned men get to live.

The hip-hop star I'm going to visit is one of around 70 men – including Scott Peterson, who was convicted of killing his pregnant wife, a pretty woman named Laci with an infectious smile, in 2005 – who enjoys the benefit of being set apart from the 500 or more other death-row men situated in the East Block of the facility. Even more famous than Peterson, the man I'm calling upon has a greater and largely sanctified status in the notorious prison. This is due in large part to both his prominent notoriety and the celebrity status of the murdered victim of his crime.

The California structure is one that I've often driven past and marveled over on my way from suburban Fairfield into the so-dubbed "The City" – a metropolis seemingly on the edge of the world. A metropolis that you better not dare call "Frisco" anymore, lest the San Francisco natives and transplants in-the-know impale you. The health-conscious, smoothie drinking and yoga practicing locals have long since moved on from that nickname that brings to mind 1970s images of discos filled with Halston-wearing, Gucci-donning cocaine-juiced players swirling women draped in Pia Rucci from head to toe across floors lit intermittently with alternately colorful lights.

That was the same decade my writing subject was transitioning from a newborn to a toddler hundreds of miles south of here, growing into a young boy who wondered at the adults drinking tall cans of Budweiser with rip-off tabs, laughing over Flip Wilson and Fred Sanford's antics in between rounds of bid whist and gin rummy that inevitably would crescendo into an inebriated adult screaming, "Boston! Boston!"

He knew nothing about this "city by the bay" back then, nor of how eloquently singers like Steve Perry, who led the band Journey, would peg this picturesque place. As a matter of fact, he'd barely traveled far outside of his South Central stomping grounds by that point – and certainly not to exotic spots in Northern California, with jewels like Big Bear, Mendocino County, Muir Woods and Cannery Row dotting the land, scenes so spectacular that they inspired writers to write and painters to paint works that would live on for centuries after their deaths.

All that sublimation and world travel would come later, when the emergence of a strange form of talking over records became mainstream in the 1980s, known as "rapping," and blasted across the country from New York over to the Los Angeles streets and neighborhood where he resided, causing him to latch onto the form of artistry that didn't require the vocal acumen of a singer, but the lyrical cadence and gymnastics of a voice box and brain that he possessed in spades.

His name is Geno Stone, better known by his famous "Geno Cide" rap name from back in the day, harkening back to lazy and weed-filled afternoons in the 1990s when I first began to listen to his rap group BWO (Bad Way Out) during my fifth and final year at Florida A & M University. I can still see the day in my mind's eye when someone popped an underground cassette tape of their raw and real lyrics into their boom box.

We college girls sat slack-jawed and amazed at the things that these thugged-out and hardened black men were saying, as if they were speaking in a mob-mentality fueled group foaming over with anger, base sexuality, and male machismo with no females present. But we *were* present, there among the handful of African-American male hangout buddies who represented "permanent fixture" student types hanging around our historically black university, grinning at the thuggish BWO group they were introducing our ears to anew.

Some of the newfound BWO fans were more concerned with copping the next frigid cold, golden 40-ounce bottle of malt liquor and the next "phat spliff" of a cigar skin packed with marijuana than the next semester's schedule, if they were still enrolled at all, and hadn't given their lives over to the incomplete grades littering certain transcripts.

While a good portion of those college-educated black men would go on to successful careers, marriages and lives, another slice would go the route of the life described and bragged about by the men in the BWO group we listened to on that day and many days following: the route that the rowdy misogynistic path would provide its main popular front man rapper, Geno himself.

§ § §

Perhaps thinking back to Geno's rough bravado, handsome face and shoulder-length locks of Jheri curls dripping from beneath his trademark black baseball cap is the reason my stomach is doing a little flip-flop right now, and not merely the gravity of the situation and writing task ahead of me itself.

I know he's definitely the reason I'm driving reluctantly and nervously in this suburban soccer mom type of vehicle towards a place filled with toughened men that I've never stepped foot inside of before. And Geno's predicament is most certainly the reason I'm interspersing his songs on my mp3 streaming through my sound system with those of the young man he killed. That deceased man is Lucas Bridgeport, better known by his hip-hop moniker "Lasso" – a similar rapper of the same sleazy genre, but from a newer, fresher and younger generation.

They say ain't nothin' new under the sun, son

But I'm the only one

Why don't you come give me some, hon?

Hon, hon, hon, hon – make it last till the dawn

Lasso's lyrics and beats are less familiar to me than Geno's as they fill my space – but the talent displayed via his rhythm, flow and cadence is undeniably on display.

It's no wonder the young maidens loved you, I think to myself. *What a waste of an epic gift.*

When Lasso's track ends my playlist shifts back to a song from his idol, predecessor and murderer – Geno. He's a man whose anthems peg different parts of my life so clearly and take me back exactly to the places I frequented when I heard them at the precise moment in time they grew from unfamiliar ditties to "monster jams" in heavy rotation. Geno formed the soundtrack to my formative years in my 20s, when "gansta rap" played an interesting background to what was going on in plenty of our lives at that period.

In my preparation to interview Geno about the man whose life he cut so short after only 23 years on this planet, I find it an interesting study to juxtapose the styles and poetic yet hateful lyrics of the hip hop heads. The derogatory names for women and phrases of fake manliness may have changed from one decade to the next to the next, but they are insulting and hurtful all the same, like a rabid dog that spawns a rabid puppy.

Bird...

Hood rat...

Slore...

Chicken head...

Slut...

Ho...

Pimp stick...

Smack down...

Trick...

It gets worse as I listen, and pick out the insults that prick like needling, gnawing hangnails. The name-calling and attempted slurs against females aren't even the worst part. It's the raging-with-hate scenarios described that remind me of why I cut off rappers like these nearly cold turkey years ago.

I tried to get with Geno's music, I really did. I even purchased it, listened to it and worked out religiously on the Stairmaster and new *LifeFitness* elliptical machines at the health club to his albums, letting that bass line pump-pump-pump-pump-me-up until the day I heard the song that literally made me snatch the headphones to my CD player off of my ears because they disgusted me so much.

Now listening to the words being said rapidly above the thumping and intricately changing beats replete within Lasso's music is making me have that same familiar knee-jerk reaction, causing me to want to scroll through my iTunes library and or hit up iTunes

Radio and flip over to anything by Da T.R.U.T.H. or LeCrae – but I cannot.

I must listen and research like a good little reporter should, especially a journalist who's been Googled and hit up by a big-time editor from *The New Yorker* and basically been given carte blanche to create a profile of the famous rapping man who killed another high-profile rapper, the same one who killed that man's daughter.

Especially a writer who sits next to a virtual pot of gold in the passenger's seat, a brown leather journal with gold gilded edges, one decorated with various words engraved along the front cover. The journal belongs to the dead woman, a young girl named Dee, a woman whose short 20-year-long life was entirely usurped by her father's 44 years, an age that matches my own. The journal of Geno's daughter darts intermittently into my peripheral vision as it bounces with the road, making it appear almost as nervous as I am, calling out on my right side like Abel's blood from the field to God, begging for some type of vengeance or understanding or purpose.

There has to be some semblance or rationale or real reason behind the senseless and violent deaths of Dee and Lasso – beyond those hinted at in "opened-veined" lyrics, cryptic diary entries and screamingly incorrect headlines made up by many a blogger or entertainment journalist who took a rumor dripped from the fingers of a random "unnamed source" allegedly "close to the situation" and ran with it to try and fill in the gaps when the man at the center of this melee wasn't saying one word that could be placed inside quotation marks.

I am fully aware of this monumental opportunity being afforded me – the fact that after all these years of sitting silently on death row, Geno has actually agreed to meet with a journalist, and the prison has consented to give me unprecedented access to the man who was himself the vortex of such a dynamic and sensational case when his death sentence was handed down that he has always had pains taken specifically to separate him from the general population for his own protection.

She said she had a gut full
I had to show her I had pull

Lasso's lyrics call out to me from his grave in a totally different manner and stance than Dee's journal, reminding and teaching me of the new generation's way of saying things, without even having to turn to Google or the Urban Dictionary at every turn but learning their meaning within the context of the terms I do understand, like learning a foreign language via Rosetta Stone.

I know that "gut full" is a crass way of saying a woman is pregnant – but going on to listen to Lasso's "The Revenge" song makes my flesh crawl with its shocking confessions.

I got her in my basement
I let my boys take her

I let my boys train her
I let my boys rain on her
Bet the bitch won't lie again
About whose seed lies within her gut full

"I'm glad he's dead," I whisper aloud, before catching myself and reminding myself that I should not think that way about a young soul who has transitioned either to heaven or hell.

"Find out if Lasso was a Christian," I speak into my smartphone after pressing the microphone symbol and taking a quick glance down at the words it has interpreted after I've clicked the "Done" button. As soon as my words appear, I click "Send" to send myself the note before me that I hold up high in my vision in front of my windshield, so that I can drive and work at the same time.

Pausing to drive slowly through the FasTrak toll lane, I accelerate onto what seems like the longest bridge in the world, with misty green hills in the distance and unseen sharks dancing below the blue skies in the choppy waters of the San Francisco Bay yards beneath my run-flat tires. White boats dot the distance as I approach another set of steel beams decorated and fashioned like so much geometry, and they put me in mind of why Geno the celebrated star turned disgraced prisoner perhaps finally decided to allow an unknown life to come to him, what with that impending death date staring him so blatantly in the face and all.

The beauty of the bay also brings a memory forth of a visit to Alcatraz Island from years ago, wherein the tour guides told our group that the inmates from yesteryear would have been able to hear the revelry, joy and laughter of the partygoers and diners and lovers having fun in "The City," seeing as though the former prison sat only 1.5 miles away.

Despite their wrongdoings or criminal behavior – or perhaps directly because of it – I empathized with what a lonely feeling they must've felt, sitting and waiting out the rest of their accursed lives on "The Rock" whilst listening to other people move on with theirs so joyfully and boisterously, each day moving at the speed of light whilst the prisoners marked the ticks of each second served with an achingly slow crawl.

"What do you miss most about being on the outside?" I speak into my smartphone after again pressing the little icon that looks like a microphone, and then pressing the "Done" button once more after the waves of peaks and valleys of my voice transmits the question into words. I send myself another text and it joins a line of others in a string that I wonder if I'll feel bold enough to ask Geno.

Stop texting and driving across a freaking bridge, Alexa, I admonish. *You'll have plenty of time to remember what to ask Geno. Just let it happen naturally.*

As I traverse over the hump that marks the center of the bridge and begin descending downward to the part that more closely meets the water, I am feeling the opposite of the relief I usually feel upon leaving a bridge and driving onto terra firma once more.

Especially once I catch sight of the prison on my left as I stick to the right lane, checking to make sure I distinguish the "San Quentin trucks" sign from the other one that points visitors like me to the expansive building that could be mistaken for a university's campus, based on its gorgeous vista and surroundings in Marin County. Ironically, it's the same county that is home to Skywalker Ranch, belonging to famous *Star Wars* filmmaker George Lucas.

Driving close to 55 miles per hour has afforded me the time to gratefully finish hearing all of Lasso's "The Revenge," a song I've decided is my least favorite of all of his that I've heard thus far. I know there's a real part of me that is simply scared of his reaction to the pregnant woman that he's cast as the antagonist of his anthem, because I've been there myself, in the place of the object of that type of male derision, but nowhere to the degree of payback that Lasso exacts upon his victim. I know it's wrong to lie to a man about the paternity of a child but thankfully I did not endure the punishment that he may or may not have exacted upon a woman who possibly did the same thing to him. Who knows if the bravado described in his lyrics is something real or fake? What if she was based on a real ex-girlfriend who lied to him about getting knocked up, and experienced the trauma of being gang raped as a result?

Instead of calling the police, maybe this nameless, faceless woman bided her time, obeying the "snitches get stitches" code of the ghetto, only throwing a slight smile heavenward when the news of Lasso's murder broke, staying silently in the shadows and remaining grateful that his wild, wayward life caught up with him at a young age.

As I veer off toward the prison, the song switches over to the familiar strains of Geno's "Blind" song, and I reach the precise lyrics that caused me to snatch the headphones off of my ears that day.

I like 'em young

I like 'em green

I like 'em fleshly

You know what I mean?

Show 'em no mercy when I come between

What is that? Is it real? Is he talking about being a pedophile or is he just bragging about some nonexistent big fakery man stance that he doesn't even possess?

I vow to ask him about all these things swirling in my head as I use my anger to try and help amp me up, repeating that "preserve my life from fear of the enemy" prayer that woke me up on my iPad this morning in Martin Luther King's voice on the "Psalm 64" song by Smokie Norful that's a lot more in line with the stuff that's promoted to my playlists these days.

I gather my notes before entering one of the most feared prisons in the nation, my mind not concentrating on the 5,400 men in baby blue and orange gear, but on the one South Central-raised homeboy-turned-superstar-turned-SMH-story now sitting on California's only death row.

Vowing to refuse to let any vestiges of Geno's charm or my school-girl crush get in the way of an objective story – although I know no such thing exists, and that most writers will include or exclude quotes and observances based on their own prejudices and paradigms galore, even unknowingly – I rehearse my laundry list of questions that disguise my complaints for the man, as I dance closer to the deadly topics of murder.

Geno must know that lyrics like those "Blind" ones are the kind of thing that drove me and a plethora of protesting others away from him and his music. I really tried, as a black woman, to support these black male rappers of a certain gangsta genre and attempted to get behind them, nodding my head to their sick beats.

I looked past the references that called us out of our names so many times; I went along with the excuses that since some women act like bitches and hos, that it was okay to call us that. (It's sad and funny how those terms have become so commonplace, reality TV women have taken to calling each other the derisive terms.) But when I got to those morose lyrics I stopped making excuses. There was no reason to continue to buy, support, back and cosign outlandish and outrageous and abusive music like that.

§ § §

"I just like the beat; I don't listen to the words," is what my husband Emanuel has often said, a similar refrain I've heard from everyone to Oprah's pal Gayle King to tens of hundreds of other people when faced with misogynist male rap lyrics.

I can understand that excuse – after all, I am a words person who knows that not everyone is concerned with lyrics. Besides, plenty of these rap songs' beats are so loud, they drown out the whispering of evil words said beneath the bass line. But once you hear it, or once you are told what is actually being said, and once it is brought directly to your face that someone likes them "great and green, young and silly" or bragging that because of him, "girls get hit then split," how can you still pour that into your vehicle in front of your children?

All of our righteousness is like filthy rags to God – yet how can I still get behind you – you Jesus-piece wearing, foul-mouthed creature? When it becomes that morbid, it's more than purely a good bass line. Who could expose their young son or daughter to such a philosophy as if to say that would be anything next to or near to okay?

§ § §

Mixed thoughts give way to complete peace, even as a prison guard tightly but gently closes me in the middle of a set of black gates with him. I notice a sign that advises people not to slam the gates. We traverse to another set of black gates and I feel a quick surge of what I've felt in the past when visiting a local jail as a writer traveling with the prison ministry team at my church. My mind's eye flashes to some kind of movie-like scene where a sudden riot breaks out before I push the vision away.

After some hubbub, I am at last face to face with the man I've seen plenty of times in music videos or television interviews. I am enthralled that he still looks good from what I immediately witness through a thick pane of glass that makes me wonder if they are tempered and bulletproof.

I'm already on edge from all the gun towers, heavy and hulking steel doors, barbed wire, metal detectors, guards with guns, dogs and other measures of security procedures I've had to go through or stole sight of on the way to get to this man – a man I'm not even sure that's worth the visit, after soaking up his stance on how he really feels about women, having marinated in the airwaves of hateful rap lyrics in my vehicle for the past hour for the drive southward.

§ § §

"Hi, I'm Alexa Coline," I say, gripping the black phone with my left hand and pressing it against my left ear, instead of thrusting my right hand out to shake his.

We are locked within cage C-13, one of twenty cages shaped like a big letter U, each a sort of claustrophobic yet comforting and romantic 8-feet by 4-feet area where all the visits to death row inmates take place – those nearby the "Condemned Row" sign, which hangs above a black gate in its strangely fancy font, as if welcoming visitors into a stage play to be performed at Christmastime.

"That's what's up," he says, jerking his chin upward quickly and back down again to acknowledge my presence. "Geno Stone."

I find it oddly charming that he tells me his full name, like when other famous people introduce themselves to peons.

Of course we know who you are already.

There are a few grey hairs seasoning Geno's black and wavy natural hair – a style that has been cut into a low 'fro that has waved *au revoir* long ago to the Jheri curls he donned at the height of his fame. His mahogany countenance is equally as handsome, barely weathered by time.

There's an odd disconcerting feeling I've felt ever since he first picked up the phone and uttered those five words in that voice that I've heard tons of times before today, both on the radio and through my headphones. It's the fact that I'm hearing those world-renowned vocals in person – live, not auto-tuned or rhyming or flowing in a suave and seductive style, nor rapping a mile a minute – but coming from the mouth directly in front of me.

Before I can get my brain to accept the connection, and reconcile these odd things, which puts me in mind of the way a person directly in front of you could be speaking into a microphone that throws their voice to the back of an auditorium, Geno speaks again.

"Today is Saturday. What if you knew you had to die in two days?" Geno asks, and stares into my opened and surprised mouth and decides to answer his own question. "Jesus knew he had to die in two days during the Passover time. And it wasn't an accidental or peaceful death neither, but one where he knew he was about to be tortured."

I suddenly find my voice to speak. "Yeah, that was when the woman anointed Christ with that expensive oil. She was a prophet in knowing he was about to die."

"Yeah," he smiles, his teeth as bright as one of those swirly CFL bulbs, the kind that can light up your hearth and home with brilliance if it's not too cold, the same ones that are a danger to you if you break them.

"And isn't it funny how Judas Iscariot was the main one complaining about wasting the oil and he ended up being the thief?" I ask.

I smile back at Geno.

Stop being star struck, I tell myself. *He is a regular person that bleeds just like all of us. Do your job. Get through this interview. Write a killer article. Win a Pulitzer Prize and move on.*

§ § §

As our conversation progresses, I think the thing that surprises me more than his in-depth biblical knowledge – (and can I pause here and parenthetically insert how great it is to see a black man who knows the word of God?) – are the multitude of multisyllabic words he knows. Sure, I expected a man who has done some hard time on death row to definitely crack open the good book and begin studying up on the things that anyone faced with his own mortality should finally study. But what I did not expect is a man from South Central L. A. – who always sported pitch black gangster regalia and snap backs, as they call those baseball caps that snap shut in the back these days, like the ones Geno wore decorated with the L.A Dodgers insignia – to know much more beyond the "pimps up, hos down" theology that his lyrics bespoke.

I decide to get right to the point. "Why did Lasso kill Dee?"

With that question, I see our open conversation begin to die suddenly before my eyes, with Geno backing away behind the curtain of his irises into a dark place that I hope he steps back out of sooner rather than later.

I need 1,000 words for this in-depth piece, and I need them ASAP.

Instead, he hangs up the phone and rises quickly, causing the prison guard nearby to snap to attention.

"I can't do this man," Geno tells the guard.

"Wait!" I holler through a dead phone, grabbing at straws until I remember to pull from my lap the brown journal that has words like Alpha and Omega; Lord of lords; The Way, the Truth and the Life; Holy One; King of kings; Son of God; Advocate; Lion of the tribe of Judah; Light of the World; Truth; Prince of Peace, and all some such other names for the Messiah and Savior decorating the cover.

I use my black handset to tap on the glass and I press the journal against the pane so he can see it. Geno looks confused, but he sits back down and lifts his receiver once more. I place mine back at my left ear as well and sit.

"Believe me, I could talk about Christ all day – I'm a Christian, too. But at some point, we need to talk about what happened."

However, Geno does not even flinch. He has set his face like flint and that hardened persona is now showing itself and even reflecting itself in his tone of voice.

"I'm willing to be completely transparent," he says lowly, but quickly begins speaking of a different subject. "Can you believe some guys do 10 years of good behavior in other prisons hoping to 'get' to come to San Quentin? Who would want to come here?"

Isn't it just like a believer to latch onto words like "transparency" but clam up when it's time to talk facts or speak about our own wrongdoings and not solely quote our favorite Scripture verses?

"Open the book," I hear from deep within my spirit, in that space above my navel, behind my abdominal walls. That's when I realize that Geno probably has no idea what journal this is that I'm thrusting in his face, the one that his ex-girlfriend Kim presented to me, using deliberate and shaky motions in between racks of sobs mere days ago in her living room, like a biological mother handing over her flesh and blood to an adoptive family member whom she knows can take better care of her baby.

Heck, Dee's own mother didn't know her daughter had kept such a journal right there in her own home, and that it held the key to the tragedies yet to unfold when the young woman penned the volatile entries.

"Had I have known…" Kim had told me, before breaking down into tears that blocked her throat and stopped her words. "If I could take away the pain."

"I know you would have," was all I could think to say in response, and hug the woman who had experienced a level of agony that no mother should feel.

It was only after Dee's funeral, when Kim found the strength to enter her daughter's room and find comfort by taking naps in her bed, drinking in the scent of her first-born by sleeping on the same pillows where Dee used to lay, that she happened across the diary, and was shocked by what she read.

The abuse.

The slaps.

The heartbreak.

The humiliation.

The pain.

All from a young man who purported to love her daughter and did his best to drop the hip hop bravado when he was around Kim – at least at first. As close as Kim and Dee were all throughout the young girl's life, bonded together like two disparate teeth making up for the space left by Geno as the patriarch, Kim had no idea of the depths of sorrow her daughter's first "real love" had caused. And if *she* didn't know, it's no wonder that Geno – miles away and busy with his rap career that paid the bills and created the fun but didn't leave a lot of room for much else in the line of fathering duties – hadn't a clue.

I open the journal and press it close and high on the glass, but not so lofty that I can't see Geno's eyes as he squints to allow the scrolled red ink on the lined pages come into view. The penmanship and everything it stands for opens the curtain again as he notices the familiar handwriting and melts somewhere from within. For the first few seconds of recognition, he keeps the hardened face, but his eyes betray his emotions and turn scarlet as the blood filtering into his capillaries draws a cherry-red map of roads atop the whites of his eyes.

I continue to hold the diary open without speaking, allowing him to lean close up to the glass in order to try to read through the tears that stream down from his left eye parallel to the tattooed tear that has been inked on the outer rim of his eye, representing the single murder he has committed in his 44-year-old lifetime. Like Denzel Washington when he starred in *Glory*, inside that profound scene where that single tear betrayed his hard won, you're-not-gonna-hurt-me persona, Geno's tears make him human once again. I know the window of heaven has opened, and we can finally begin to talk about his daughter Dee and everything that led up to her death and beyond unhindered. At least I hope we will.

"It's like Dee is talking to me again," Geno says. "It's a sign. I didn't think I'd ever get the chance…"

"You're not dying in two days," I say, "but we don't know if your execution date will be soon. Please don't take your story to the grave with you."

"I don't want to talk about my case," he says quietly, honestly, while using his sleeve to wipe away what still must be viewed as a betrayal of a well-honed image of a strong male. I can tell he is grateful for the company, but he is still holding on to the last traces of his hardened hip-hop façade, as if he's already given me way too much too soon by breaking down at the start of our interview.

"Okay," I say, pulling a hefty three-ring binder full of the rapper's printed lyrics over in front of me with my right hand until they land squarely between us. I am subconsciously grateful for all these special allowances I've been awarded as a researcher and writer to bring with me on the inside, when I know full well that others have the most seemingly mundane things confiscated from them during their visits to see loved ones behind bars.

I flip and fan through many pages to get to the beginning, a page with a song title printed in larger, bolder text above its stanzas of lyrics. "Let's talk about 'Public Punany' then."

The jolt of the striking change of subjects causes Geno's head to lurch backward, as if someone has slapped him in the forehead with an open palm. A slight, melancholy-like upward lifting of the right side of his mouth makes a memory emerge from somewhere way beyond the walls of the room where we now sit.

"Tell me how you and Pastor Prince came up with that one," I say, resisting the urge to flip on the small voice recorder that I've also miraculously been allowed to bring inside and hold it up in a clunky manner near the phone's earpiece. That would be way too awkward, and there's no way I want to break this coming flow of words by issuing the standard "I'm recording this conversation" warning mantra now, right when Geno might start singing like a canary.

"You know Paul, too?" Geno asks, incredulous. "He wasn't Pastor Nobody back then."

"I haven't met him yet, but I've done my research," I say, glancing down at my handwritten notes with a list of names.

"I see. That was my boy – *road dog, boss hog,*" Geno breaks into a rhyme that can't help but send us into chuckles, despite the seriousness of the previous moments. "Man, he was always trying to keep me in line."

"How'd you meet him?"

"Back in high school. I was about to kick his butt 'cause I heard he'd been talking all this jazz about me – saying I was weak and stuff. Turns out he was just mad over some bitc—chick." Geno catches himself, putting a hand over his own mouth before changing his lingo.

"So what'd you do?" I ask.

"I rolled up in his face," he says, giving off a tone that says, '*What you think I did?*'

I smile and remain quiet, leaving room for him to continue.

"But it was funny, after that, we just became tight. I told him, 'Man, don't let anybody punk you like I did."

We again laugh at the irony of it all – meeting your best friend by confronting him in that way. As he talks, I continue to study Geno, taking more mental notes than physical ones, listening for the words that jump out so strongly it's as if they are bolded and floating in the air – and I know they will become words that make it into print somewhere.

It's no surprise to see a black man whose last act of violence captured and put him inside the prison walls wherein it practically forced him to become a crazy criminal or a Christian, get yoked in the yard, grow bulging muscles and know his Bible inside and out, however it's not every day that you're privy to a superstar rapper who has killed another superstar rapper who killed his own daughter – and is now facing his own death date.

This should be some story.

"Paul, man…" Geno grins again, hesitating as he begins to recall some sinister secret. "We used to just kick it back at Taft, talking to girls in the hallway."

"Taft High School," I nod and whisper, more to myself than to Geno, who is already lost in the memory.

"He's a pastor now, but back in the day, boy…he was worse than me with the females."

"Tell me," I urge, my gaze falling to the wicked smile gracing his full lips, my eyes zooming in towards the gap made between in his front teeth, soaking up the way he forms his words as if I'm wearing telescopic contact lenses.

"*Smack myself up,*" returns the familiar rap refrain to my brain, and instead of literally smacking my own face, like when Cher smacked Nicolas Cage in *Moonstruck*

and commanded of his lustful, lovelorn state to "Snap out
of it!" – I shake my head with such a goofy, violent
motion that Geno notices.

"You all right?" he asks.

"I'm straight. So what you're saying is that Paul
was a worse 'mhore' than you?"

"A what?"

"A *mhore*. You know, man whore. I thought I made
it up, like Shakespeare made up words. Turns out it's
already in the Urban Dictionary."

"Well, I'm not exactly up on all the latest lingo,
being holed up in here and all."

I glance down at unnecessary paperwork to avoid
his gaze. "I can teach you."

"Bet," he says. "So yes, Miss Alexa, I was a big-time
'mhore' back then."

"*Ms.* Alexa," I correct quickly, adopting a serious
tone once again. "But thanks for not calling me 'Ma'am' –
I hate that. Let's get to it. And by the way, not only are
you not going to die in two days, you're not Jesus."

I don't want my words to hurt him, I am only trying
to return back across the line to some semblance of
professional writer interviewing her article's subject
matter – even though our pupils, irises and retinas have
already locked for several uncomfortable seconds of
silence, punctuated by our breaths overlaying any other
immediate racket in the room.

It's been mere minutes since I laid eyes on this
Geno Stone – but we've already crossed the unspoken

line where things have shifted from the professional to the personal.

"All right, *Mizz* Coline," Geno says with exaggerated emphasis, and I'm impressed by the fact that he's taken the time and interest to remember my last name.

As his words transport me to the halls of the William Howard Taft Charter High School miles and miles south of us down in Woodland Hills, I'm suddenly existing like a fly on the wall in his world decades ago, as if I'm watching the action he describes unfold before me on an XD Extreme Digital Experience auditorium 38-feet tall by 70-feet high movie screen.

I want to, but I can't look away.

Chapter 2:

School-Dazed and Confused

Paul and Geno are a sight to behold as the duo joke and "pimp walk" with an exaggerated gait down the crowded hallway of their high school. Paul is gaunt and tall, his stark white crocheted head-to-toe outfit highlighted by the silver stethoscope swinging from a long black cord around his neck.

"MC Paul MD in the house," he croons to the girls who part down either side to let the boys pass, as if they are two Pharaohs gliding down the mighty Nile River.

"I'm telling you man, we need to start our own rap group," Geno counters, himself dressed in a pink and white striped shirt whose ample collar has been flipped upward, allowing the ends of his California curls to brush stains of moisture onto the fabric. The first three opened buttons of the shirt display a thick gold chain dancing among the hairs of Geno's chest, and a brilliant cubic zirconia stud earring peeks out from among the curls from his left earlobe. "That's where it's at."

"Where we gon' practice?" Paul asks. "You and your mom's place is too small and can't take no noise. And you know the 'Good Reverend Doctor Daddy' ain't having that stuff up in my house."

"Aw, you ain't saying nothing but a word, homey," Geno says, his eyes moving from Paul to a cute and petite girl standing alone against her locker, one who returns his lusty gaze.

"What's up with you today, Slim?" Geno asks, sidling up to her, putting his arm around her shoulder. "Those are some poppin' Guess jeans you got on."

She smiles. "It's Kim. You forgot my name already, huh?"

Geno cuts a quick and knowing look toward Paul, who covers his mouth and turns away to laugh.

"Naw, baby, I could never forget a body as fine as yours."

Geno gives her the elevator eyes right in front of her face, causing his own eyes to take a slow ride up and down the length of her body, not pausing or trying to be incognito at all with his flirting. "Tell me, are your parents gonna be home after school today?"

"No, it's just me and my mom, and she works till midnight every night," Kim says, chewing her gum and smiling, folding it into air pockets on the side of her mouth between her cheek and teeth, popping the bubbles with loud pronouncements. "What'chu need?"

§ § §

"That's how I first got with Kim," Geno says through the phone, looking up into my face and away from his long held memory that has brightened his expression in the way that recalling the joy and rush of first infatuations can do.

I am taken aback, or rather, forward, snapped back into this present day, grasping the next sensible question out of the ether that a woman lost in the haze of thirstiness might ask a dynamic man like him, who has opened a little more of his vulnerable soul.

"What attracted you to Kim when you met her...or when you finally remembered meeting her..." I laugh, in spite of myself.

Geno gets it. He laughs, too. "You gotta understand, it was so many girls – *fine* girls – back in the day." He pauses. "And afterward."

How much further afterward? I want to ask, but stop myself.

This is why women fall in love with prison dudes, those who couldn't be tamed while free to wander in the street, loud and defiant, the rolling stone type whose "feet never stay at home" but were "now in the street, now in the square," releasing the nectar of their loins in public every day at the homes of varying women – women who felt lucky to have the stud darken her doorway, if only to go no sooner than he came.

However, in jail – correction, maximum-security prison – with their limbs at times shackled, these playa-players are finally, literally, on lockdown. They are no longer swimming in a sea of estrogen with many different choices of body types and personalities to fulfill their specific perceived need for that day, be it one woman who's a great listener, another who is excellent in bed, or another whose home they drop by often to get a plate of food because she cooks so well, just like their grandma.

No this California Casanova's attention is focused in on one female form in front of him who does not wear prison guard garb or yell at him to fall in line. Only a thick glass now here, right in my face, separates the overabundance of Geno's charm. His voice is pressing into my left ear, the funnel for a concentrated mass of charm in the flesh, nearly as powerful or even more so than the days when it became a clarion call for sex to millions of us dumb little girls who sang his anti-female lyrics by heart and repeated misogynistic rants with a charming smile that made us forget all the hate directed at us as a species.

But that womanly world has largely been one out of touch – literally and metaphorically – for him behind these walls; especially since death row inmates have less contact with the outside world and are more isolated than others. This is even more true in Geno's case – seeing as though his fame became a prison of its own making when he first arrived here, and for quite some time following. It's true that a lot of the inmates showed him love, specifically the ones of his own generation. But there was also a dangerous subset of men that were more loyal to Lasso, and über-pissed at Geno for taking the life of their current hip-hop idol

I feel his mental, emotional, spiritual and sensual hunger in the weight of his stare as Geno tries to explain his ruthless style as a youth to me.

"So talking to girls in the hallway of high school..." I say, trying to return to the topic at hand. "That's how you honed your womanizing skills."

"Well, yeah," Geno looks down, halfway ashamed, as if he's never let a woman see this honest side of his game before. "I guess I learned it from my father – when he was around."

"Your parents are divorced?" I asked.

"Yeah," he says, growing solemn. "But Kim, she was more than just another honey to me. She was something special. I guess I wasn't ready to settle down, though."

§ § §

"What about H2C?" Geno asks Paul, as they stand in a compact garage next to large silver turntables balancing perilously atop black speakers next to blue crates filled with old albums. Geno points to the crates brimming over with records and says, "Hip Hop Cratez!"

Paul shakes his head. "Naw, man, that's played. What about D-Fi-Ant, you know, like Sydney Poitier in that old joint, *The Defiant Ones?*"

Geno balks. "We need something better. Something nobody has and that everybody can remember."

Paul pulls a random album out of one of the crates and lays it flat on its side. "Why don't we take a little inspiration break?"

Geno digs in his pocket and extracts a small manila envelope of marijuana. "A'ight man, but I can't keep dipping in the supply man. You know this is our way out."

Paul pulls out a slim yellow package from his wallet, with "Top" written in blue font above a multi-colored logo of a spinning top with the words "Fine Gummed Cigarette Papers" below it. With deft expertise, he licks the sticky end of one paper and glues it to another to achieve a perfect rectangle.

"It's also our way *in*," Paul says, snatching the small bag of weed from Geno. "Gimme that *bo*."

"Whatever man – that's the last nickel bag we're smoking tonight," Geno says, patting a bulging chest pocket in his Members Only jacket. "The rest of this phat stack is going to straight-up customers to be turned into straight-up cash…"

Paul chimes in, "…to start our straight-up record company."

"*Getting high off our own supply*," Geno rhymes, watching Paul dump the marijuana out and toss the stems and seeds on the ground.

"Boy!" Kim's voice comes out of nowhere, echoing in the garage so that her shrill shrieks are amplified. She bends down to rapidly pick up the evidence. "Don't you know my mother could find that?"

"Sorry little lady," he apologizes. "I didn't mean you no harm."

Geno motions to Paul to hurry and finish rolling the joint, which he does, as Geno pulls Kim to the side and sweet-talks her mood from anger to delight.

"Kim, slimmy cakes, what your *moms* got in the fridge?" he grins, speaking softly and smoothly.

"We got a little somethin' somethin'," she smiles back, speaking equally as smooth. "She taught me how to fry chicken this past weekend. First you dip the wings in egg whites with a whole bunch of Lawry's seasoning salt and then you put 'em in flour and get your grease really hot—"

Geno's eyes widen as his mouth salivates. "You got all that in the kitchen now?"

"Yeah, you want me to make you some?" Kim asks, batting her eyelashes.

"It ain't even a question. You know I do. Let me go blaze these flames first – and you know we gon' have the munchies after."

"I know," she says. "But take a walk with that stuff. You know my mother got a nose like a bear smelling something in the woods from miles away."

"Peace!" Geno shouts, smacking Kim on the fanny. "I'll be back for dessert, too," he winks.

Kim giggles and wiggles as she walks out of the garage toward the kitchen, and Paul pounds Geno's fist under his own when she is out of earshot, when the duo of males breaks into loud laughter.

"I got to give it to you bro," Paul says. "Your pimping skills are immaculate."

"I learned from the master, right? Now blaze that blunt and stop popping off your gums. Homeys before hos, *brauh.*"

Paul lights up as the men walk past small colorful homes with black gates across their windows and heavy frame doors on most. By the time their walk takes them to the busier intersection of Crenshaw and Florence, past laundry marts, gas stations, Chinese food eateries, lottery signs and a McDonald's, the large joint is now a teeny roach.

"It's mine, man," Geno says, tossing the blackened marijuana butt into his mouth and swallowing it.

"You can have that, man."

Geno laughs high and loud, uncharacteristic of the stance he'd normally take in public, in the busy section of a town where image is everything. But a radio station billboard looming high above their heads transfixes him.

"We gon' be up there one day, man, I'm telling you," Geno tells Paul, both of their eyes red and swollen, but their intentions serious.

"Then let's do this," Paul says. "*Straight Flesh.*"

The duo launches into a rhyme they've obviously rapped quite a few times before, so fast and in sync is their rhythm:

Road dog, boss hog

Keep that bond, flip that mon'

C-dub love

Till death, brauh

Suddenly, both young men are stunned into silence when a group of men and women, five in total, trot on large brown horses down the sidewalk across the street. Their mouths fall open at the sight.

"Man, what'd you put in this stuff?" Paul asks, panicking, not trusting his vision. "*Whatchu* decide to try out on me?"

"Nothing, man. Stop tripping! You know I don't mess with that *yayo*," Geno protests, still staring at the curious group on horseback that draws the attention of honking cars and amazed passersby. "See – other people see them, too."

"Well I've seen it all now," Paul says, as they continue staring. While stopped at a corner with traffic whizzing by, one man stands atop his horse and does the snake dance until he loses his balance and jumps down to the sidewalk.

"What kind of day is this?" Geno wonders aloud.

§ § §

The intersection has grown less busy and the after-dusk sky has darkened, but Paul and Geno are still loitering around the front of a liquor store when a new-modeled Jaguar approaches slowly and pulls close to the curb.

"Is that 5-0?" Paul whispers, straightening up, taking his hands out of his pockets and adopting a stance whereby his big feet prepare to either plant themselves stronger or launch into a full out run.

Geno squints, bowing his head low and moving it back and forth in a bob and weave motion until he can spot the driver better. "Chill, man, chill," he reaches out to calm Paul. "That's ol' dude from last week who copped that bag off us."

Paul looks again. "No it ain't! Wait, man..."

Geno walks up to the car as the passenger side window is lowered and though he's initially taken aback, he plays it cool. "You know I got that *'green-green'* – you trying to get one of these bags up off me?"

The fortyish African-American man takes one of the small bags that Geno thrusts his way, opens it and smells it. "Yeah, that's it – you must be Geno, huh?"

Geno looks surprised. "You know me, man? I know *you*!"

"I sent one of my boys to get some last week. We were *throwed*, dog, for real," he says.

Geno laughs. "It's good stuff," he says, then takes all the bags out of his stuffed pocket and throws them on the man's passenger seat.

Paul grows wide-eyed. "What you doing dog?"

"You call yourself being in the game?" Geno asks Paul, smacking his chest hard before bowing back low to face the man in the car. "This is DV-U$, the big time producer."

"Y'all can call me Jeffrey on the low, since your weed is so good," he says.

"I'll tell you what," Geno says, lifting his eyes so Paul will catch his drift. "You can have all that on me for free, and I'll bring you an ounce if you let us spit this freestyle rhyme in your ear right now."

Jeffrey exhales. He's heard it a billion times before. Taking another deep inhale of the bag, he relents. "Go on, spit a verse or two."

He halfway listens as he scoops the bags on his passenger seat into a briefcase below, but as Geno's superior flows start rhyming meticulously over Paul's beat-boxing, Jeffrey pauses, taking notice. These are not the everyday kids who stop him on the street, thinking they'll miraculously turn into the next big rap star.

"What's your group's name?" he asks.

Geno and Paul look at each other, stammer, and laugh.

Jeffrey shakes his head and digs in his pocket, extracting a $100 bill and a business card.

"Tell you what fellas," he says, handing the money and card to Geno. "Go home and figure out a good name, then give me a call in the morning so you can shoot by the studio. And bring that ounce you talked about."

Geno opens the bill and stares at it in his hand. Paul grabs the card and rubs his finger across the raised lettering as he reads it.

"Welcome to Cell Block H Records," Jeffrey says, rolling up his window and taking off.

Back in the garage, Paul and Geno are still incredulously giggling and laughing, all pretense of bravado and brave manhood gone.

"When you threw that entire stash of weed on his seat I was like what the—" Paul recalls.

"I can't believe you didn't know who he was from the *get go*," Geno says, pacing, unable to sit down. "Now we need to come up with a name and we'll be straight."

Paul paces in circles around the garage, too. "We already straight, man. We got a record deal! It's our way out."

Geno holds the $100 bill high up in the air and waves it like a flag on a windy stormy day. "*This* is our way out the ghetto."

"A sweet way out," Paul says.

"The *best* way out," Geno says, his eyes falling on the album cover that Paul had absentmindedly pulled from the record crate earlier to roll the joint on. It's like Geno sees it for the first time, that white album cover with the name MICHAEL JACKSON in thick black capital letters of text streaming down the right-hand side, the word *Bad* appearing in red, as if strategically spray-painted by some rebellious prankster to overlay the name.

"A *bad* way out," Geno says.

"BWO!" Paul shouts, getting it.

"*Bad is good – and good is all bad!*"

They shout and rhyme in unison, giving each other chest bumps and wrestling themselves to the ground.

§ § §

"So that's how BWO was born," I say, cutting a glance over to my blank notepad and all my recording devices that are turned off. I'm at peace, not filled with panic, though, a calm ease telling me inside that I'll remember the bulk of our conversation.

"Yeah," Geno says wistfully. "Ain't it ironic how something so extraordinary can happen on ordinary days? I mean, all these days you prepare and plan, wondering if it's ever gonna happen for you – begging somebody, anybody, to put you on – and then, boom!"

"It happens," I say.

"It becomes this gigantic conglomerate of a project or record that you think maybe in your gut that people might love, but when it's just you and your thoughts, you have no idea if it'll be another due-paying stepping stone, or..." he trails off.

"Or if it will be the biggest-selling multi-platinum success that has come out of this area," I finish his thought.

"Exactly."

Those are the same thoughts I was just thinking; it's like he can read my mind.

I begin jotting down words in messy penmanship strictly to escape his heavy stare. *Geno has had plenty of practice with this woman-wooing business of his. I won't fall prey to his schemes.*

He is an anomaly before me, a roughneck from South Central LA (before it was scrubbed of the "Central" wording and still existed as a hub of racial animosity) who waxes philosophical about supremely intelligent things you wouldn't imagine or expect. This isn't the image of the hardened gangster who sold crack and held rocks in his hand under a lamppost while looking out for the *po-po* back in the day, as his lyrics claim.

This man is an inner-city ghetto poet, with a brilliant mind and tender soul, only betrayed once in a while by an incorrect tense or turn of phrase such as "*I seen* that girl before."

I let my reverie fill the small spaces we occupy, and assume these pregnant pauses will be necessary for our conversation. I might as well make the most of all the extended time the prison has provided me to speak with this man, and now that he is letting me gently unravel his life as if I'm unfurling the delicate angora yarn that's been set in intricate directions around a mysterious spool at the core, I want to continue along in this vein, and not let go until the secret in the middle is revealed.

"So what did Kim think of your record deal?" I ask.

"Oh she was ecstatic," Geno pauses, "at first. But that's when our surprise arrived."

§ § §

"*Don't be fooled, you're my tool in this quiet storm,*" Geno raps along with the radio, while attempting to replicate the scratching sounds he hears with records on the turntable in the garage.

He is alone, but before long, Kim slides her feet across the oil-stained flooring, causing a loud swishing sound. She looks afraid to approach Geno, who pulls his large black headphones off of his ears when he sees her.

"Man, if I could just sample that beat," Geno says. "I know Jeffrey would sign us for real once he hears that type of demo."

"You'll get signed," Kim says sadly. "It's probably already a done deal. He just don't wanna give y'all that 50-50 split you asked for."

"He should," Geno says, with his ample eyebrows furrowing as he looks at the downtrodden state of Kim. "What's wrong with you?"

Kim breathes out, long, hard and noisily with an exaggerated moan. She pulls a foreign-looking white stick from behind her back and twists it up in the air with disdain. "I'm pregnant," she admits with a finality that prepares itself for the worst.

"For real?" Geno says, standing up, curiosity all over his expression. He comes near her – she flinches. Geno is befuddled by her reaction but reaches out to examine the stick anyway. "So this means 'pregnant' huh?"

Kim flips the box over in her hand and shows him the explanatory legend with photos. "Yep, you see – pregnant." She points from the photo to the real-life window on the stick. Geno studies it, flips it, looks back and forth from the photo to the actual test strip in his hand.

She waits expectantly for his reaction, hesitating, until she can no longer take his quietness any more. "And before you even ask, yes, it is yours."

Geno looks at her with genuine surprise. "Of course it's mine – it better be mine! Who else's would it be?"

"Nobody's!" Kim shouts, but then quiets down as she looks outside of the garage, checking for nosey neighbors. When she sees none, she continues, in a much softer but more resolute and reasoning voice. "All I need is $200 and I can take care of it – I already called the abortion clinic for information, but they needed my mom's name so I called—"

"Wait, what you talking about?" Geno asks her, instinctively taking the box from her hands and putting the stick inside, grabbing it closer to his chest.

"You know what I'm talking about. My friend Charlotte went to this clinic downtown and got her abortion for $200, so I was going to go to the same place," Kim says.

"Without even talking to me? What if I want to keep it? This is my baby, too," he says, his voice growing angrier.

"Well I didn't think you would want it," Kim says, thrown off by Geno's reaction. "We're still teenagers – and when you get your record contract, you'll be off on the road and stuff."

Geno grabs his forehead, as if he is trying to pull the words from his brain. Finally, he gets down on his knees and clutches at her thighs. "Please, Kim, please don't kill our baby. I promise you, I'll take care of you both. I'll do what I have to do."

Kim falters, her balance thrown off a bit by Geno pulling at her legs. He reaches out to steady her as she puts her hand on his shoulder to steady her body as well. She looks upward at the ceiling for answers.

"I don't know, Geno," she says, "I don't want to be alone. I love you. I'd love to have your baby. Just not now. My mother's gonna kill me."

Geno searches that same ceiling for answers, and when one comes to him, he grabs a spindle adapter from inside the middle of a nearby 45-rpm record and tries to place it on Kim's ring finger on her left hand, but when he realizes the hole in the center is too small, he lays it on top.

"I promise you, when I get my record deal, I will turn this into the fattest diamond you have ever seen," he says, causing a huge smile to break through the tears that have streaked both of their faces.

"*Geeenooooo*...." Kim says.

"Will you marry me?" he looks up and asks, begging, gripping the flesh of her forearm as if he's a man sinking in the ocean holding on for dear life.

"You'd better be for real," she says, shaking her head, but then finally letting out an exasperated, "Yes!"

§ § §

"The best laid plans…" Geno breathes hard, letting out a saddened moan.

"A man's mind plans his way," I concur.

"That's what Paul always used to tell me, especially after he got saved," Geno says, still a pinch or hint of a trace of abandonment flashing across his face.

"What year was that?" I ask.

"I remember the exact *day*. It was November 5, 1988. The day I signed with Cell Block H Records," he says.

"Alone."

"Yup, alone."

§ § §

Here I am again, driving, searching for more. And I don't know exactly what that "more" is right now. If someone were to ask me why I'm driving the winding and twisting roads that make up the Pacific Coast Highway, beyond and through that famous Devil's Slide area I've always read about, taking in the intermittent beauty of the powerful and brooding ocean off to my right-hand side down toward Los Angeles, I don't know that I'd have a good response at this time.

I don't know why, I only know I must talk to Pastor Prince.

It's a great writing gig, for sure – at $1 per word – almost unheard of in this penny-per-page view online era – it's nothing at all to scoff at, even with my curriculum vitae. But something other than money is driving me along the twists and curves down to Pastor Prince's Haven of Love Church, a feeling and inclination so strong that neither Geno nor my husband thought it strange when I said I wanted to take the weekend to trek down to LA to do further research before writing the article by talking to the pastor.

Especially as I watched Geno speak so fondly about his longtime "road dog," but not so perfectly as if not to cover up every crack and crevice caused from the thick-as-thieves duo parting ways when Paul made the early choice in life to follow his calling into the ministry, leaving Geno to follow his calling into the rap game with other cohorts.

As Geno recounted what he felt was a devastating choice his best friend was making at the time, I couldn't shake the feeling that there was so much more to the story that I needed to know, or some other unforeseen reason I needed to lay eyes on this man myself – and hear his testimony from his own mouth.

§ § §

Haven of Love reminds me of plenty of other mega-churches I've attended over the years, each with its own little quirks and specialized sayings that make it unique to its specifically ensconced little group.

That is why I am holding my thick, faux leather covered Bible above my left shoulder in the air with thousands of others right now, catching on as they repeat in unison, "This is the Word of God."

The windup, the denouement, they are similar to my own huge church back home. Though the loose structure of the same heights of emotionalism make their appearances throughout Pastor Prince's sermon, it is not manufactured like I've seen too many times these days.

"And I tried hash in high school and everything," the pastor tells the crowd, notably standing on the floor and not the stage – speaking in a normal tone of voice that precludes yelling and a "sing-songy" style that other men in his position might adopt. "I was going the wrong route, but God snatched me up and saved me, and showed me the right way."

After the sermon has ended, the offering has been taken and the benediction given, I stand in the long line of mostly women waiting to speak to Pastor Prince.

I, unlike the others, am not standing for a turn to ask the man of God to pray for me or my husband, or to help me figure out if I should leave my church and come to his. No, this visit has been prearranged, and I am delighted that the pastor has accounted for his time once I meet him at the front.

"Sister Coline, yes," Pastor Prince says after hugging me when I re-introduce myself. "Brother Solomon is going to take you right into my office to get you situated. I shouldn't be too long, I hope."

I survey the long line of people behind me, some no doubt with pressing prayer needs. "Take your time; thank you!" I call out, as I am whisked away into the inner sanctum of the church.

I am grateful for the time alone that "Brother Solomon" provides once showing me to Pastor Prince's office – and am tripping out that I'm even in the man's office at all, a virtual stranger, trusted with such a private place. I mean, it isn't the man's home or anything, but the photos of his smiling wife and cute kids decorating the room prove to me that he is exactly as open as he seemed during the sermon. There's no false pretense or the need for a lot of fuss in order to get to this man – an attitude keeping right in line with the accessibility of his sermon. Pastor Prince simply relaxed and *talked* to us, not like a man putting on a show for God, but one who earnestly, fervently and honestly believed in our Maker and his power.

§§§

"*Converted*, but not perfect," Pastor Prince says when he's finally "come down" from the heights of the day's activities and falls back in his high-backed chair to talk to me. "That's how I'd describe Geno's salvation story – that's how I'd describe any of us."

"I hear you," I say. "Just a sinner saved by grace, right?"

"That's right on," he says, pointing his finger at me while placing the other one at the tip of his nose. "Geno didn't understand it when I gave my life to Christ – nobody did."

"Well you were so young," I offer.

"Yeah, it was like one minute me and my boy were about to turn into these huge rap stars, and then the next minute, all they know is that I'm carrying my Bible to school, trying to find a ride to church," he laughs.

"I can't imagine," I say. "When I was in high school and I'd see people reading the Bible on the city bus, I'd wonder, 'What are they reading that for?'"

"That's what people asked me. Then they asked, 'Did your mother die or something?' They just didn't get it," he says.

"Not at that time, but Geno eventually got it, right?" I ask, somewhat confused as to what Pastor Prince was saying about the state of his friend's soul.

"Geno's salvation moment came after his brother got killed," he says. "That seemed to trigger something about his mortality within him – but he was already deep in the rap game at that moment. I mean, look what he did, he went out and made that horrible 'Don't F With my MRS' song afterward, and then got up there and thanked God for the Grammy!"

"I remember watching that," I say, "but I wasn't even saved yet. I didn't think anything of it. It's funny how different you look at things from the perspective of your belief system at that point in your life."

"And thank God for growth, huh?"

"Most certainly."

"But still, he continued to do the wrong thing in life – and look where it led him," Pastor Prince says.

"There's hope, right? Even Moses killed a man, and God still used him to lead a mighty movement of people out of bondage."

"That's true…" he says, agreeing with my theology, but sensing something deeper in my interest about Geno's case. "Tell my boy I said hi and that I'm coming up there to holler at him soon."

"Will do," I say. "Will do."

§ § §

I feel it. The flow has returned. I knew there was a reason to drive all the way down the Pacific Coast Highway simply to get a face-to-face meeting with Pastor Prince, if anything merely to hear his version of why he dropped out of the record label deal even before any pen ink was put to paper.

"I didn't feel right in my soul," he'd told me, and it was another one of those quotes I could see dancing through the air in bold letters, preparing to land in a word document to be shipped off to my editor soon and very soon.

It wasn't that I was lollygagging on Sunday after church after I made it back home at last, falling in and out of sleep on my huge green sofa in the living room by the big bay window as my husband sequestered himself away watching football in our bedroom into the wee hours of the evening. Instead, I was marinating on Geno's story about all the things that he had told me during that first visit and everything that Pastor Prince let me in on in my talk with him.

So by Monday morning as I walked around Muir Woods, staring at the ancient trees, everything that needed to pour out of me began pouring out of me in gushes, like all the thoughts and rush of feelings that had been poured into me over recent days had no other outlet.

My writing fervor returned and I knew the flow was there. I spoke words into my smartphone and emailed them to myself, and as I said them out loud I could feel the power behind them pushing them out of me and into the bottom microphone of my phone translated by the voice-to-text feature with a power beyond this earth.

The flow is here. Right now. This isn't merely some article or piece of writing that will be a flash in the pan with no hits and soon forgotten and buried beneath one billion other blog posts and articles.

This one is special. I can feel it in that space that forms the two lines of my upper abs. There's an electricity in my gut that tells me this writing assignment will be different than all the others. I will see it on the movie screen, even more so in reality than the movie screen life of Geno playing out before my eyes as he spoke to me at the prison.

I read and reread it aloud to myself, clicking the "Spelling and Grammar" link on my top toolbar one more time before finally closing the document and emailing it to my editor. With both hands first splayed on the screen as I say a silent prayer for God to bless it tremendously, I reach down and maneuver my track-pad, hovering over "Send" and then resolutely clicking it with surety.

§ § §

I hope this is a good enough excuse to return to San Quentin. After all, I've printed out the copy of the article about Geno with its "100k" next to the Facebook share button, and a 57k Tweet count, just in case the prison officials changed their mind about me bringing all the devices they said I could bring to the inside.

"Unprecedented access." That's the term I keep hearing about my visits with Geno, so I know it makes sense for me to come back – even if I tell myself it's only because they said this time I could take even more photos other than the quick snaps that accompanied the profile that they must've loved.

He's just messing with me now, I think to myself, trying to position my smartphone's camera lens in a way that makes it through the spaces in the metal covering his prison cell.

Yes, I said his prison cell.

I've been allowed to take a mess of images of Geno in his "natural habitat," the place where he spends a good 19 out of every 24 hours of each day.

"I think I got it," I say, hoping my hand shaking like a leaf in the autumn wind doesn't betray my nervousness at being this close to him in his state of being. It's not the small size of his living quarters that is causing me the most disconcertion at this moment, nor the fact that other prisoners I witnessed on the East Block were sending letters to one another in the form of flying white kites that floated around – ones which my paranoia told me were notes all about me – or other paraphernalia being snaked around on makeshift fishing lines through the well-lit space.

"You all right?" Geno asks.

There's an orange glow in his cell, uniquely made by placing paper over his light, giving it an ethereal halo.

"Yeah," I say, feigning complete interest in the line of photos I've just taken, scrolling through them with my index finger as I swipe my camera roll.

It's a bad move, because the images are forcing me to look at the very thing that's making me uneasy, which is Geno, and his bare-chested state of being, having lounged around in his boxers in his cell, showing me the contents of his room and posing as I took impromptu shots to accompany – what next – I do not know.

He knew I was coming here today. I refuse to ask him to put on some clothes. He did this on purpose.

"Do they look good?" he asks.

"Do you want to see?" I answer, and we both draw closer to one another. "How can I do this?"

Geno opens his food port and thrusts his strong arm through the hole with precision. I place my smartphone with the purple sparkling case in his hand, using my other hand to wrap his around the phone, making sure he has a good grip before taking it into his cell.

"You got it?"

"Yeah," he says.

"Just scroll through like this," I instruct, making the motion of swiping my fingers.

"That's *all right*," he says, not like in a boring way, but with emphasis and an accompanying smile that says it's a job well done.

"You look good," I whisper, and I catch more kites in my imagined peripheral vision, sailing upward from the first floor to cells unknown. The place seems unusually quiet, except for the two of us.

We linger. I give him time to scroll all the photos he wants to see, even those of innocuous things like the animals I've come across in Muir Woods, or other nature-like shots that I've applied Instagram filters to and made look incredible.

He is taking me in – all of me, the quirky nature-loving writer-girl in front of him, well past the time her assignment with her subject is supposed to be completed. He flips my smartphone on its back, marveling over the cross I've painted with red nail polish surrounded by a heart on the back, nodding with approval.

"I like to distinguish my phone from others," I stammer.

"I see," he says. "Have you ever thought of making this your logo?"

"Wow...the Holy Spirit is working overtime today. I thought the same thing earlier this week."

When Geno stretches his hand back through the food slot to return my phone, I allow my fingers to gently grab his all the while making sure my smartphone doesn't fall to the ground. He leaves his arm distended for what seems like forever – reaching, grabbing for something else beyond his reach. It would be so easy to step closer to his grasp. I mean, there it is – right in front of me. That well honed, serious sexual "it factor" that drew the attention of millions of women away from his other group mates to make him the rising star of the group. And it hasn't faded that far away over time.

God help me have the power to resist this. I am a married woman. And beyond that I'm a bondservant of Christ. I can't let anything get in the way of this mission and task I've been blessed to receive and cover.

The loud beep of a text message breaks into my thoughts, vibrating the sinister lustfulness of my meditations away with a jolt. Geno watches as my eyes grow wide when I scroll up through a very lengthy text message my editor has sent over.

"Alexa, what is it?" Geno says, smirking without even knowing what he's elated about.

In that same manner that missing puzzle pieces finally fit together, or the one ingredient needed to make a recipe a family favorite finally falls into place, the message in that text at last lets me know what all the driving, sky-staring and typing has been about over these past days.

"We got a book deal!" I exclaim.

"What?"

"They love you, Geno," I explain. "Your fans miss you and can't get enough. It's like they want to know more and more. I guess we're going to have to do a lot more interviews," I say, smiling. "They want this thing published by Christmas."

Geno walks to the back wall of his short cell, flaunting his pectoral muscles like a peacock. "I guess you're going to need a lot more of my time," he surmises, like a devious schoolboy concocting a plot to hook up with the Homecoming Queen.

"I believe I am," I say. "Let's get started. There's no time like the present."

"Ask me anything you want, Alexa," he says.

"Tell me more about when you guys first hit," I say. "You know, when you first got put on."

"Me and Paul? Oh yeah, after we met Jeffrey, he put us to work! He had us working like a couple of Hebrew slaves," Geno says.

I crack up and instinctively follow him with my gaze as he paces the narrow cell exactly like a caged animal.

"DV-U$ had us performing as the opening act at local concerts as well as competing in statewide talent shows, rehearsing for days, anything that would get us used to being in front of audiences and make our flow tighter," Geno recalls, smiling.

Geno's words become the voice-over to the images now playing in my mind. The movie of Geno's life enters its second act.

§ § §

The marquee reads "Talent Show" outside the entrance of the Los Angeles Convention Center as a bunch of buzz and hubbub brings noise and excitement back stage.

Paul and Geno wait in the wings while a girl group does a routine across the black stage, with its faded and peeling paint, to a house music type of song.

"We can't change it at the last minute!" Paul is incensed.

"I'm telling you man, I can feel the audience man," Geno says, peeking out at the crowd, who seem delighted enough with the girls on stage. "We gotta get 'em amped. We gotta go all out if we wanna win this thing."

Paul peers around Geno's head to the front row to spy Kim. "You know your girl's out there, right?"

"Which one?" Geno laughs.

"All right. I warned you, man."

"In life, there are some risks that are worth taking," Geno says, then launches right into his routine on stage, before the girl group has even left the stage and is still gathering smatterings of applause.

"I'm rocking all the hos, I'm getting all the pros," Geno busts out on stage, leaving Paul to catch up with his antics. "I thought I told you though, I'll even school yo' ho..."

Paul is more of the hype man that Geno doesn't even need, for his self-assured bravado has won over and awakened the crowd – even the group of girls who have unwittingly become his sudden stage prop objects like so much pretty set decoration.

As Geno continues to literally spit into the microphone with vapors of mist, because he is rapping so hard and with such ferocity, there is one figure in the front row that isn't standing and cheering and fist pumping like the rest of the crowd.

It is Kim, sitting stone-faced and angry, scowling at Geno, who purposely will not look at her as he works the crowd and reads the room for all he's worth.

§ § §

"And the winner is..." says the muffled voice spilling from the auditorium, pausing for extra effect. "B-W-OOOOO!"

Kim leans against a classroom door in an all but deserted hallway, rolling her eyes. Time passes, and a few rowdy teens here and there pass her by, including a group of males.

"You need to drop that fool," one of them says to her, grabbing his crotch. "Come on and get with a fly guy like me!"

The group of young men laughs, until Geno comes around the corner, lugging a big gold-plated trophy and walking with Paul.

"What'd you say, man?" Geno yells, lurching into an angry sprint after the culprit.

"Wait, Geno, wait," Paul says, running after him.

Geno runs in full speed past Kim, who remains in her position, clutching her stomach as the group of guys take off running down and around the corner.

Paul turns around and spies Kim's hazardous condition and calls out to Geno again. "Wait, man!"

Geno pops out of his angry pursuit long enough to turn around and witness the fact that something is not right with Kim. He sees Paul trying to help Kim, but pushes Paul out of the way when he reaches them.

"What's wrong, baby? What's wrong?" Geno asks, still gripping the trophy and trying to tend to Kim all at once.

"You're what's wrong!" she screams. "Rocking all the hos? Really Geno? Am I one of your hos? Is our baby one of your hos?"

Geno looks around, embarrassed. "Hold that down," he says in a loud whisper. "Let's get you some fresh air."

He reaches out to assist her by holding her upper arm, but Kim pulls away from him.

"I got this man," Geno tells Paul. "I'll get back. Holler."

Paul reaches for the trophy. "You want me to take that home?"

"Naw, man, you can come visit her at my crib," Geno smiles. "I told you we was gonna beat out that other rap group and all those wack dancers."

Paul wants to smile, but notices Kim growing angrier at Geno's jubilation. "Just handle your business man, handle your business," he says, giving Geno a quick chest bump before leaving.

Inside Geno's huge classic cherry red 1964 Impala, Kim's anger is coming out in bursts of tears. "So you're rocking all the hos and getting all the blows, huh?"

Geno looks outside his driver's side window, away from Kim, so she can't see the upward turn of his lips. "Those are just words, man."

"I'm not a man!"

"Kim, sweetheart, mother of my child," he softens, "I make that stuff up to sound good."

"You're a liar," she cries. "I already heard my girls telling me things about you."

"What girls? What things? You know people always trying to start some mess. They just jealous."

"It's you, Geno. You're the one making a fool out of me," Kim says, calming and shaking her head. "And you begged me to have this baby and everything. Now I feel so trapped."

Kim quickly tries to open the passenger side door but gets confused and panics because it's locked.

"Where you going?" Geno asks, grabbing her forearm tightly.

She turns around with a look of fear on her face, shaking her head quickly and pointing to her mouth.

"Oh!" Geno says, reaching past her to unlock the door and open it. As he does, Kim leans her body out of the oversized vehicle and pukes all over the parking lot ground.

§§§

"So you were cheating on her!" I say, like a detective from a *Dateline NBC* show who has solved a mystery.

"How'd you know?" Geno asks, furrowing his brows at my astuteness.

"Kim got sick; a woman knows," I say. "Even though she was pregnant, a woman still knows. It probably wasn't all morning sickness."

"Well, I didn't even know she was about to get sick – all I knew was I didn't want no earlin' in my '64," he says, turning on the charm, making us both laugh out loud again.

I swear even the nearby guard chuckles.

Geno notices and leans in to me.

"They liked the piece you did," he whispers. "It really put the prison in a better light and gave them some good press. It really showed how much they improved some of the conditions here, or at least the bright side of things – if you can call it that. Like all the volunteers and programs and stuff."

"Whatever gets me closer to you," I tease, adding, "and gets a great book out of it in the end."

Chapter 3:

Now I'm in the Big Time

"This place ain't no joke," Geno tells me as soon as I sit down in a barren interview room across an old table. "This is the place no one wants to live."

He is more pensive, thoughtful and serious today, on the day I've returned, gripping Dee's journal once more, eager to dig into the heart of the story of her life with her dad. I temper my mood to match his, wondering what has happened to dull his senses so much since our last visit.

"The first time I heard those gates shut behind me, man," he says, "I knew it was real."

"I can only imagine," I say, only putting myself in his shoes for a split second, thinking of how trapped he must feel inside a place I can eventually walk out of – after going through the same checkpoints that brought me here.

To Geno, this castle is a fort on a 275-acre piece of land near the San Francisco Bay that he can't enjoy, like those Alcatraz bad guys from the days of old. It's a place to rehearse the mistakes made and wrong turns taken over and over again. San Quentin is a place where – if you are a special writer visiting a special inmate under special private custody on death row – it's worth it to get your smartphone confiscated along with your wallet and driver's license and transport yourself through various gates to get to a subject with quite the story to tell behind his guarded eyes and shell-shocked soul.

"Okay, are you ready for this journey?" I ask Geno, tempering my naturally upbeat nature to match his seemingly downtrodden mood. "Let's start with the beginning of this journal because we have a lot of ground to cover by Christmas."

I carefully flip open Dee's journal to its wrinkled and tattered first pages, pressing the middle seam up and down until it almost lays flat, but I still hold my hand across it to keep it open as I prepare to read a passage.

"I hate this place," Geno suddenly speaks up. "All the bars on the windows, the shanks, the danger...you can't even run unless you're on the basketball court."

As much as Geno was moved to such depths of emotion, to tears even, when he saw Dee's journal, right now he's acting like he doesn't want to read it at all.

I follow his lead, shifting subjects suddenly.

"Yeah, the guard told me they don't even let people take hostages. They said if you grabbed me, they'd shoot right through me to get to you," I blurt out, wrinkling my nose at the green stab-proof security vest that covers the ugly green scrubs I was given to cover my "non-regulation" linen clothes.

"Aw, yeah, they would. Trust and believe."

I am only somewhat surprised by Geno's change of heart, being a student of human nature as a writer, and all of the anomalous and contradictory ways that our emotions can take us.

"So what's your favorite rap song?" he asks.

More dodging.

I study the ceiling as if I'm trying to decide upon an answer, when in reality, I'm trying every journalistic interviewing tactic I've ever learned to get this man to open up about his daughter.

What could have happened in the interim from the previous visit to this one? Perhaps while I was gone Geno has gotten the notion that Dee's diary may contain some passages that he's not yet ready to read, some things that would shatter the image of his innocent little daughter to smithereens. Beyond that, perhaps he already knows in his deepest innards that the voice of his daughter and her experiences with him – or the lack there of – can't be disputed.

Dee isn't some journalist pontificating from afar about their relationship, but she is one birthed from his own loins. Her testimony can't be – or shouldn't be – disputed. After all, this golden book of words I hold in my hand, that I long to read aloud to her daddy, is one that the young woman never intended for him to see. It is an expression of her feelings toward a man who doesn't seem ready to face facts in red and purple curly-cue ink on lined paper.

So as I press gently but methodically forward, imagining ways to let him know what his daughter has said, I stall by answering his question – making him think he is getting his own way and controlling this interview fully.

"I don't know, man," I say, frowning and contorting my face. "Rap didn't used to be so out of control. It didn't start off as a woman-hating, misogynistic genre of music that sought to debase and deride women."

"Yeah, I feel you," Geno agrees. "The Green Hill Gang and them were all about having fun."

"Or even when it was more serious, it began as a way for folks in the ghetto to speak of their plight to people who would never enter a ghetto."

"True dat," he says.

"But to answer your question – my favorites from back in the day were just those little moments in songs when I'd hear a verse and I'd have to ask: *Who is that?*"

"Like who?" Geno asks, and I realize it's a moment for one artist to feel the competition from a fan of another artist.

"Like Mischievous Mics…" I answer, counting on my index finger.

"You liked them?"

"Yeah, when I heard those lyrics about them never knowing their dad—" I stop myself. Everything leads back to Geno's non-existent relationship with his daughter, without me even trying to directly broach the subject. I quickly ramble on, hoping to make a circuitous route back to the actual journal under my hand, open and splayed on the table, waiting patiently for its day in court before time runs out.

Geno and I talk on and on about our memories of rap, like a couple getting the small talk out of the way before trusting each other enough to get to the meat of the meeting. We talk about how hip-hop exploded with such a force to be reckoned with that even Saturday Night Live created a popular skit that repeated rap lyrics – a big thing back in the days when SNL wasn't even known as "SNL," and the "not ready for prime time players" included folks like Chevy Chase and Bill Murray – before Kenan Thompson and Jay Pharoah were even born.

§ § §

The guard shifts on his feet, his chin lifted and eyes forward, but ever aware of our every move. Both Geno and I know we are running out of time, despite the extended hours the prison has specially granted us for these unprecedented interviews. I no longer want to seemingly waste any more time – although I know none of this backstory and small chit chat we've been making is going to waste. It is all grist for the mill in what will become Geno's first authorized book version of his life story.

But enough is enough. It's true you can lead a horse to the water, and that you can't make him drink. However, a soft tone and the perfect Holy Spirit-led timing can help nudge his muzzle down to the refreshing waves of the river.

"So, do you want to hear about the time Dee met Lasso in a club on the Sunset Strip?" I ask, offering a sympathetic closed-mouthed smile that is hopefully letting him know I'm treading carefully toward his tragic situation.

Geno exhales loudly and deeply, sitting up in his chair and steeling himself, as if he's some ancient warrior soldier placing a heavy breastplate in front of his chest to prevent deep stab wounds.

"Yes," he says through his mouth, although everything about his body language and stature says no.

I jump at the opportunity, hunching down and speaking distinctly and softly before Geno can tell me to stop reading. As I begin reading the poetic and prolific section of the diary verbatim, the bland and boring room fades away, and we are transported into that same club with a thumping beat and pulsing strobe lights where the path of this man's daughter's life – and eventually his own – would be changed by one hook up.

§ § §

I know who you are, Lasso told me as soon as he walked up to me.

I knew it. I wondered if that was the reason he passed over all of my other girlfriends and made a beeline for me, only because he knew my dad was the famous Geno Cide. Just like all the other people who have tried to get close to me once they find out who my father is. But little do they want to hear my sad story, when they realize that although I have his name and his nose and his big feet and mahogany skin, that's about all that my dad has given me.

Oh yeah, and the check – the monthly check that he gives to Mommy in place of his presence, not presents, as if they can make up for all the time spent away, for all the embarrassing questions that people ask when they get down to letting me know they really want front row seats to his concert, not to become my real "ride or die" friend.

Only when they continue to press, and based on who they are and how close I feel to the person, will I finally admit that I rarely talk to my dad. Outside of those conversations that are brief and about the weather or when we laugh over something really stupid and inane that proves the shallow nature of our relationship, we have no deep or in-depth conversations between us. I have more of those with my best friends. They know much more about me than the great "Geno Cide" that everybody loves.

That's when I tell some of the chosen few and they learn the awful truth about my famous rapper dad, idolized by many a young man and loved by young girls swooning over his lusty lyrics and amazing flow. That ugly truth is that I am not one of them. I'm not a fan. SMDH. I hate him for abandoning us.

But when I looked at Lasso tonight, I realized he was different. He's famous himself, on his own. He ain't one of those cute dudes necessarily looking for more than I'm willing to give because they have nothing on their own. The playing field is level with Lasso; he could've easily picked one of my girlfriends, but for some reason he picked me and all I know right now was that I was feeling so dejected and rejected by my own blood that it felt good to finally be picked out of the crowd of girls by someone rough and rugged like my dad, someone that Geno would probably hate. *The competition.*

After all the times I've turned dudes down – 1,000 times saying no to 1,000 different men and women who tried to get closer and steal a piece of my soul in stolen moments here or there, for some reason I finally said yes. To Lasso, of all people.

I know a million ways to turn somebody down gently or more forcefully, telling them it's not them but that it's me, or when I'm in a really mean mood and a person doesn't get the hint, telling them that it *is* them – it is *all* them – but tonight none of those rejection rehearsals needed to come into play when Lasso scooped me up and carried me to that hidden section of the VIP bathroom suite.

We giggled when his sagging pants began to fall so low down his thighs as he walked, so he had to walk all wide like a duck. My only thought was not saying no or "put me down" or nothing like that, but I was hoping that my 148 pounds felt really light in his arms.

"He could get it for real," I thought, "and I'll bet you he knows how to put it down."

Pretty soon, I forgot all about any worries about my weight and tripped out that I was smashing at last. I had Lasso.

Hmmm...Dee Bridgeport sounds good enough to me. A lot better than the last name I inherited from Mr. Big Stuff Stone that I hardly ever see. What was that Geno rhymed about on his first album that I'd sneaked and listened to – even when I was hypocritically not allowed to listen to my own father's rhymes because they were supposedly too dirty for kids?

Oh yeah, that's right: "She let me hit it on the first night. I know she's tryin' to take that first flight..."

Little did Daddy know that not only were all my friends listening to him spit stuff like that when we were as young as 8 years old, but that we internalized it – and we girls learned what we had to do to bag a man like Lasso. So Geno can't say nothing to me about this – if he ever cared. Shoot, I learned to act this way from him.

§ § §

Dee's break in writing for that pivotal day is the perfect place for me to take a sip of water and a break in reading, an optimal time to gauge Geno's reaction to such a heartbreaking moment.

My peripheral vision caught sight of him shifting around uncomfortably as I recounted word for word the tale of his only known daughter losing her virginity to an up and coming rapper, but I'd kept my head down and plowed through the reading, pretending I needed to be really close to the words to see them. In reality, I wanted to dig at least through this passage before the day's end – and get some kind of reaction out of Geno, the epitome of male bravado being punched in the gut with the fruit of his labors.

"I remember when she was a little girl, and I took Dee and her friends to go see one of those *Home Alone* movies," Geno says, an odd memory to unveil after what he's just heard.

I nod and smile.

"They loved it. It was the part where little McCauley Caulkin asks the robbers, 'Are you ready to give up? Or are you thirsty for more?'" he continues.

"Dee shouted, 'We're thirsty for more!' She was so cute with all that hair in those pigtails...I took them all to Chuck E. Cheese's and everything after that in a Lincoln Town Car. I was so worn out..."

Geno gets lost in the memory, but at the same time looks down at my hands as if he's hoping this is a memory that I will definitely track in the book, as if it is proof to counteract the fact that he had abandoned his daughter, and instead make it appear that he was more present than he really was in real life.

"About how old was she then?" I ask.

"I don't know," he says. "Maybe five or six."

We understand without saying it aloud the real recall of the incident exactly for what it was, one of those times whereby Kim already told me that Geno as a father fell through town in between busy tour schedule stops, when the groupies and the weed and the cocaine and the 40 ounces couldn't touch that part of his soul that called out for home.

It was one of those times when Kim laid aside her anger at him and his absence long enough to understand the importance of Dee needing to be near her father and she allowed him to come scoop up his daughter and a few friends in the fancy Lincoln Town Car and show them a fabulous time out for toddler types on the town. For him it was thrills, grins and fun and no fevers, no 2 a.m. feedings, no ordinary daily frustrations of life filled with raising kids.

"She was my sweet baby girl," Geno whispers, his voice cracking and halting to get the words out.

That is why Geno is having such a hard time accepting the fact that Dee gave up her virginity finally so easily and readily on the first night she met Lasso. Geno wasn't privy to the day-to-day adjustments that present parents get to experience with their children.

For 24/7 types of moms and dads, the five-year-old girl turns six and one day you notice new words and extensive vocabularies or fresh and firsthand skills that you allow yourself to get used to in a gradual way instead of your mind being stuck on the image of the five-year-old in pigtails enjoying a *Home Alone* movie, perpetually innocent and in love with her Daddy.

No, day-to-day parents have a front and center seat to her accolades and accomplishments at school. They know about the day she cried over a friend not speaking to her at school because she was in a bad mood or the day she rejoiced because her drawing, the product of hard work, got published in a national magazine. They were there for the highs and more highs and prayerfully not too many lows – but they sacrificed the time and spent those hours attending award ceremonies and those recitals. They came to realize the sacrifice of time was well worth experiencing the growth of their child firsthand. "I had to make the money," Geno explains with a shrug, as if he knows himself as soon as the words drip from his large lips that it is only a half-truth. "I had to take care of my family. A man who doesn't support his family is worse than an unbeliever, the Bible says."

"I know, she knows," I say, trying to make him feel better, although we both know that there are other musicians who find a way to have successful musical careers and maintain their marriages and parenthoods in a smoother fashion.

I contemplate if I should flip back to an earlier time in Dee's journal, in her younger teen years. Avoid it as much as he might want to mentally, Geno will have to face his daughter's thoughts by hook or crook eventually, and the fact that she had problems with his career and parenting skills. That 16-year-old girl who grew into an 18-year-old girl who entered her 20s without much of a relationship with her own dad is forever trapped in

Geno's mind as the five-year-old with a sweet smile and lonely eyes and long ponytails.

"But my sweet baby girl had fun that day, boy," he says, turning on the smiles and charm once more to mask the pain. "Dee was sleep before I even got back to Kim's house."

Geno's words make it known that he's trying to do the impossible: He wants to turn back time and make up for everything he missed to somehow bring Dee back to life in the process, a feat that only God could accomplish.

He is non-responsive to his own daughter calling him a hypocrite in her righteous anger. Rappers like him may think their lyrics aren't harmful – I mean, they certainly pay plenty of lip service to that serious question in interviews that challenge them – but they turn right around and disallow their own kids to listen to their music. They know it's harmful.

Besides, Geno has manufactured all these memories in his mind of many special times with his daughter that, as proven by Dee's journal, just didn't exist. Perhaps it's basically too difficult for him to face the fact that random girls and groupies and chicken heads and hood rats and everything else he called the women who so easily went back to his hotel room and did either him or his boys or both – after all, "I'll only come if my homeys can have some!" – they all got more of his time than his own flesh and blood.

All these years later, as a man in his mid 40s, Geno is still holding onto the last remnants of swagger that doesn't want to admit personal failings to his fans and see his behavior in print of those failures. Gangsta rap isn't about failure, it's about overcoming, getting over, and there's no room for the image of a deadbeat dad – even if it's only emotionally deadbeat and not financially deadbeat – in that carefully crafted portrait of a strong black man done wrong by society.

"Listen," I say so softly and womanly and gently, all the while stopping myself from reaching out to instinctively touch his hand. "We've all done things wrong that we wish we could go back and change. But maybe there is a way you can make it all up to Dee, everything you wish you could've done, just by telling her story – and yours."

"Okay," he relents. "No holds bar. I didn't realize Dee was all engrossed and involved in my lyrics like that."

"A lot of kids were. Still are," I say.

Both Geno and I soon realize that this is more than a mere book that we are creating, so help us God, it's a movement, and it will take longer and go deeper than we both anticipated. But it's worth it, because it's bettering souls in the process.

§ § §

Geno and I are climbing stairs from the cellblock area with an armed guard, a ruddy mess of a blonde concrete spiral staircase with a silver handrail. The promise of hopeful light filtering from above through the shaft bespeaks of something interesting to come. I have no idea how much.

During the previous visit, I complained aloud about needing to get out of those stifling rooms before I went crazy, then thought to myself how silly I must've sounded saying that to someone who has spent years inside the same location.

Lo and behold, the third visit to this maximum-security prison has now brought about an unexpected vista.

"This is the North Seg's yard," Geno tells me when we hit the top of the stairs and are led onto a roof with a stunning view of Mount Tamalpais from the west.

"Oh my Lord," I breathe it all in. "You get to come up here?"

"Yeah, a lot of dudes get a lot of free reign for good behavior over here," he says, grabbing a nearby basketball and spinning it on his index finger. Geno becomes the lone player beneath a basketball hoop that he lobs shots toward, with one after the other sailing through the rim, a practiced play of perfection.

Geno looks down at his blue shirt, as if instinctively to offer it to me, like a man on the outside automatically seeking to remove his dinner jacket to give to a lady. There is an impossibly picturesque background as the afternoon sun begins to fade.

It's not every day that a top official of the California Department of Corrections and Rehabilitation lets anybody in these parts. Only one outside interviewer has ever even spoken with death row inmates kind of like this – until now. I know good and well that the text I read on the official website in a long list of media rules stated, "Inmates may not participate in specific-person, face-to-face interviews."

My sheer presence here negates the fact of what I've read. The events that have transpired, including the runaway success of the article, and now the wide door of opportunity for a book deal, still has me feeling like I'm existing in some sort of dream-like state, one I want Geno to help me understand.

"Why do you get special privileges?" I ask. "Where is everybody else?"

My query stirs something in him, something that makes him begin to dribble the ball as a distraction.

"Some people would consider me a 'prize' in here," he says. "You know – they'd want to break me off, and I don't mean in a good way."

"Oh," I say, the vision of prison-made shanks and other weapons I witnessed during my research of San Quentin by watching National Geographic specials on DirecTV prior to meeting Geno flashing to my mind. I let it go.

There is a tense atmosphere that's palpable in this place, similar to Geno's song, "Bitches Delight." It's one of those things that people long to touch yet repels it at the same time.

In reading Dee's journal last night, I learned that Lasso was one of those rap stars who she never thought she'd find attractive in that manner until she met him in person, nor did she ever expect to be one of the women in his line of vision, especially considering all the exotic and gorgeous females he had dated during his short lifetime.

But that was a different lifetime from the life sentence planned to end in death for her father, unlike the one Geno has spent behind solid walls, beneath gun towers and the watchful gaze of an entertained guard. The tables have shifted. The worm has turned.

"So tell me, what did your family think about your songs?" I ask, gathering invisible notes in my head that will make up some semblance of an award-winning background chapter on this superstar's life.

"My Gran-Sadie hated it," he says, and while registering my confusions, he adds, "She was my favorite grandmother. The only grandmother I ever knew."

"She found my book of rhymes and told me I could do better. She said a real man didn't need to use all those 'cuss words' to get his point across," Geno recalls, mimicking an older woman's southern twang.

"Aw, she sounds sweet."

"She was. I'm from a good stock of women," he says. "I couldn't hear her though. I told her I had to go with that hard persona because that's what was selling back then."

"So the rap bravado wasn't really you?" I ask.

Geno pauses, taking time to articulate his real answer. He's not manufacturing a lie nor digging for euphemisms to "pretty up" the truth. It's a move I appreciate, especially as I hear the realism in his answer.

"I don't really know if it was me or not," he says. "At first it was more about me playing a role – this hard lil' gangster. You feel me? But then I couldn't really tell anymore what part was me and what part was not."

"It melded together," I say, joining my fingers into an intertwined state. The diamond on my left ring finger sparkles in the light. I catch Geno looking at the stone, which brings to mind one of those questions I'd spoken into my smartphone before I met him. "Didn't you ever want to get married in the end?"

Geno glances down at the diamond-shaped space made between his legs as he props them open. "Not at first; not with Kim," he says. "I only told her that so she would keep my baby."

"Dee…" I say, cautiously mentioning her name for the first time this visit, hoping it's an entrée into discussing another pivotal page of her journal with him.

"Dee, yup."

He presses his lips together and considers the dark mountainous range in the distance and keeps speaking.

"Kim wanted to get married so *bad*," he says, emphasizing her desire with length and intonation on the last word. "But my career was starting to take off. And by the time I was ready to get married, it was too late. I was in here and she'd moved on."

Sadness hangs heavy in the air.

"It's never too late," I say, wanting to etch some level of hopefulness into his situation, if only for one night, if only in his dreams. Instead of reading Dee's next section of words to Geno, I take a break and allow the memory of his sweetheart to come forth, back when Dee was still a baby and her mother a young woman begging to be important in his life.

All of a sudden, as he speaks, I realize that Geno is taking the slow progression forward, allowing each scene to catch up to the memory he holds in his mind of Dee still being a young girl.

If this is what it takes to get the truth out of him, I'm down.

§ § §

"Why can't we go with you?" Kim asks, propping herself up on her elbow within the fluffy white down comforter decorating the hotel bed.

"You can't take no baby on the road," Geno says, getting up out of bed to light a Newport cigarette and stare out the window down to the street below.

"Who says? It's not like Dee is in school or anything. She's a baby."

"*Exactly*," Geno says condescendingly, as if speaking slowly to a child until they get the lesson. "My tour is going all the way to Paris."

"That's why I want to go with you, maybe we could elope over there and throw those locks in that river," Kim smiles.

"What? I ain't got time for all that. I'm gonna be working. Getting this paper. Stacking these dead presidents," Geno says, and throws a stack of one-dollar bills all over the bed, letting them float over Kim. "Making these *ins*!"

She is not amused. "You said you wanted to marry me, Geno. You said you were going to be there for us. It's bad enough you weren't even there when Dee was born."

"I was making money!" Geno protests. "Besides, your mama held your hand during the delivery and helps you with everything you need – and you can stay right home with her until I get back."

"Don't expect me to wait forever."

Geno is taken aback. "Where you going?" he asks.

§§§

So this is how it will be, getting snippets out of him when I can, like a dentist gripping and twisting and cracking and breaking a wisdom tooth to extract every last piece of enamel out of the bleeding gums without damaging the nerves.

I stand and stretch, curving the arc of my back to find comfort. I know my time with Geno is winding down, but there's so much more to the story that I want to know, that I want to suck out of his soul in one fell swoop, like a juicy novel that's full of anticipation and intrigue.

Help him feel the love You still have for him, God, I pray.

"Well, enough of the sad stuff for now," I say, brushing my lower pant hems. "Tell me about 1993, when 'Public Punany' dropped."

Geno laughs at the recollection.

"Who inspired that one?" I pry. "Not Kim, I presume."

He adopts a sort of pimp-like gait and speaking pattern. "The female form can inspire great art. You know how we do," he quips. "Or used to do, rather."

"I can imagine. But why don't you tell me anyway."

"I was on a worldwide tour, there were groupies everywhere, just throwing it at me," he says. "How was I to say no?"

"Like this: 'No.'"

"Oh, you got jokes?" he laughs.

"Now tell me more about Kim before they kick me out of here."

"I was running around the world doing my *thang* – and she was back home in L.A., holding it down and all, raising our baby girl while I was getting that paper."

"How often did you see her?" I ask. "Both of them, I mean."

Geno stops dribbling, and turns to brooding again.

"Not often enough. I know that now," he says.

It is a breakthrough in his admissions, and I want to get as much out of him as possible while he's in this truthful mood.

"So don't hold back," I say. "Tell me about the tour. Tell me about the girls."

"Aw, you don't want to hear that. Although I do still have some rowdy pictures left from those days."

"I don't think we can publish those," I say. "It's not that kind of book."

"Well you know, I mean, what can I say? We were young and wild," Geno confesses, looking sheepish.

"It's funny, everybody who was famous talks about how young they were and wild in those touring days. I mean, I watch a lot of that show called *Life After* on TV One. Have you heard of that?"

"Yeah, but I haven't peeped it yet," he says.

"Anyway, most people talk about being wild and what they claim was a state of being 'free' and having all that sex and all these groupies and stuff. But the ones who are the most honest tell the bad side of it too."

"Oh yeah, *mos def*. There were consequences to my behavior," he says. "I've seen some dudes, they took it too far. A lot of my homey's ended up dead, or..."

"In jail?" I ask, barely above a whisper, but the thought had to be completed.

"Yep. Just like me."

With that one statement, I know that Geno is at last ready to broach the subject of Lasso, that he's giving me the green light to start skirting the edges of a story that no one else dared to delve too deeply into with him, lest they feel the wrath of the rapper.

"How did you meet Lasso?" I ask, kindly and in a matter-of-fact manner, ready for him to nod to the guard at any moment and return to the safety of his cell, away from these probing questions.

"It was still back in the '90s, and I didn't even know I was seeing that little superstar till he told me years later."

§ § §

Geno is on the set with DV-U$ on Rosecrans in Compton as he shoots the original "Left Coast Love" video with another rapper. Cameras are rolling and Geno is doing plenty of preening and posturing for the crowd of futuristically dressed guys and dolls all around the set, either as extras or onlookers.

On his mother's shoulders, watching the amazing *Mad Max Beyond Thunderdome*-styled video set is a 7-year-old boy named Lucas.

"He was only a couple of years older than Dee back at home," Geno's voice from the present scene says over the action from eons ago. "Not that I'd taken the time to fall through that time and check on my baby. I was too concerned with getting that video in the can."

Geno makes a "raise the roof" signal toward Lucas in the crowd, and Lucas makes it back.

§ § §

"You know, that's when he told Dee he decided to be a rapper? At that exact moment in time. How foul is that?" Geno asks.

"What's foul about it?" I ask. "I heard he adopted the moniker 'Lasso' because he wanted to rope your record sales."

"I heard that, too," Geno says.

"And he blew up so fast," I recall. "Lasso's demo even went gold."

"I know, right? It took a long time for BWO to hear our song on the radio," he says, sounding jealous. "We weren't like EMC or some group that heard our song and began dancing around the car. "

"Hmmm..." I say, "I don't know why they wouldn't want to play 'Public Punany' on the radio." We laugh.

"But they put us on after a while. After we hit gold they had to recognize we were a force to be reckoned with," he says.

"You certainly were," I agree. "You certainly *are*."

"Look – I'm just trying to redeem myself. A lot of rappers that came up with me need to redeem themselves, too. They should at least apologize for the damage our lyrics have done to society."

"Like who?"

"Shoot – Chill EP and Freeze Z...I was rapping with all those dudes before they blew up and switched from rapping to big-time acting."

"Ooohhh yeah, I loved them!"

"Why do good girls like bad guys?" he asks, and I realize he is actually asking why his daughter would fall for a guy like Lasso without coming out and asking it directly.

"From what I've read of her diary, Dee liked Lasso because he was confident and manly," I say. "She saw him as her protector."

Those last words are like a jab at Geno's heart, so I quickly recover with something he may like.

"But she thought her stepdad was weak," I counter.

"He *was* weak," Geno agrees.

"She wanted a guy like you, Geno," I open the journal once more to find her exact quote. "You were her mother's one true love. Lasso was only her validator. She was like a moth to his bad flame because of her low self-esteem."

Geno hangs his head. "I should've been there. That guy who was like me ended up filling that void and killing her."

I can say nothing in the face of this revelation, but only let the quotes float in the air until they can land on my fingers and onto the backlit keyboard of my computer as soon as I get home.

§ § §

"That's why they put full-length mirrors in clubs," Geno says, apparently turning over in his mind the night that Dee met Lasso. "Women like to watch themselves."

"Yeah, that's what my husband says about me," I say, wanting to probe more into his brain, but I know that I've already gotten enough out of him for the time being for a thick and heavy chapter.

Besides, I can tell by his shortened responses that I've pried too much. I've gone too far. I remind myself to take baby steps with this man, and once again go back to the light-heartedness in order to progress.

Geno and I straighten, wordless for a while, taking in the circumference and full spectrum of what has occurred. That's when he says something intuitive – one of those quotes that float like words into the nighttime sky that will follow me all the way home and dance around my dreams.

"They can take my body and lock it up, but they can't lock up my mind or soul or spirit," he says, profoundly.

"Keep it that way," I say.

All the way home, I drive and consider the pinkish black sky and hills, acutely aware for the first time that there is a man – lots of men, but who am I kidding, my mind still centers on the one – who does not have the freedom to see as much of this same night vista of stars that I seemingly float through right now. I have the freedom to walk straight out of the sliding glass door within my master bedroom and consider the constellations any time I want – even if it's three in the morning.

Geno can't witness the "PRECARIOUS" sign that's been mowed into the green hills near my home, as a warning to stay away from dangerous things that could hurt you.

I remember the day my brother-in-law said they should carve something more apparent into the hill, like "Danger!" for the folks who didn't know that precarious meant that was one shaky hill to stand on.

It's odd but foreboding that all these thoughts combine as I think of what I'll write about my interactions with Geno in his book – but I find it even more compelling that for the first time, I foresee an ending where I want him free – free to see this same night sky that I see, any moment that he desires.

As we get closer to the real-deal of his life story's plots and sub-plots, I have a feeling that I won't be the only one who wants him out of those prison blues and living a life that doesn't involve bars or anything close to lethal injections.

Chapter 4:

Miss Movin' On

Seeing Geno is becoming easier, like going to see an old friend. An old friend who sits on death row at San Quentin, that is. One could never or should never get used to a place like this.

"I got my degree from USC," Geno says as an icebreaker to our newest conversation today, before we rummage back through the hard details of Dee's journal once more.

"Really?" I ask, making an impressed mental note of his higher education.

"Yeah, from the University of South Central," he quips. "My street degree. Imagine going from the hood to the top of your game. I'm talking having enough 'ish and power to rent out Chasen's in 1992 on Grammy night!"

"I'm not from L.A. – what is that?"

"It's a restaurant that not many of *us* could afford to book that night," Geno explains, rubbing his index finger down his forearm to indicate his dark brown skin color.

"The invitation we sent out was a summons talking 'bout, 'You are hereby ordered to appear...' and stuff. My homeys were probably scared as hell when they got that one," Geno laughs at the memory.

"Creative," I mention.

"Yeah, when you got enough green…" he now rubs his thumb against the other four fingers on his hand, "…you can do almost anything."

"So is that what you did at the top of your game?" I ask, fiddling around with the journal, hoping to open it soon and get to the pivotal night that brought Geno to this place. "Did you do almost anything you wanted?"

"I tried," he looks down and admits, rubbing the scruffy five o'clock shadow of a goatee on his chin with his left hand. "We used to tell the groupies they had to get naked right there in the hotel hallway, before they could go any farther."

"'You better juke or get your drawers took,' huh?" I ask.

"Exactly."

§§§

Geno is stalling again.

"It seemed like forever till our Cell Block deal went through," he says. "We tried to get a P&D deal with the big guys and our manager shopped other deals, but it all fell through at first. Even the distribution deal."

"A P&D deal?"

"Pressing and distribution," he explains. "Nobody wanted to take a chance on us besides Jeffrey, but he had enough pull to finally get us put on. And then we took off, and everybody who had rejected us wanted a part of us."

I search my brain to remember the research I'd read. "Well, not everybody. Some of those big record companies were still scared of y'all, with all that talk about hurting women and then that shooting that happened in the studio."

"Those were just some jealous dudes trying to scare us," Geno says, brushing off the incident. "The main thing I learned around that time was that we had signed some slave deals and we didn't know no better. We didn't know nothing about owning our masters and publishing. That stuff really matters when you start talking about going double platinum, getting $5 million for 50 million copies sold."

Geno seems to be getting lost in the details of his deal, straying from the main crux of the story that all his readers will want to know, chiefly, what were all the emotions he experienced on the night Dee died, and how did they lead up to him killing Lasso?

Perhaps I can use what he's yammering on about to get him to the heart of the matter.

"Do you ever think about all those 50 million copies not just being numbers, but see them as people – as families – listening to your lyrics?" I ask.

"Hell yeah," he says, his mind already turning, his facial expression giving away the fact that Geno's wondering where this line of questioning is going. "It was the right time, and to sell that much music was amazing. The streets were thirsty for it, because our stories weren't being told. We hit that underserved market."

"Indeed," I pause, thinking of a way to take the heat off of him and redirect my questions as if I'm being self deprecating. "My thing is, when I see 100,000 hits on one of my articles one day – I think that's cool, especially thinking about all that advertising income."

"I bet. You've got to show me more some day," he says.

"I will. But I had to stop and think to myself: Those aren't just 100,000 hits or numbers – those represent *real people*. And some of them are probably kids. Then I think: What am I dishing out to them?"

We pause, letting the air go quiet on the phone that serves as a speaking mechanism between the thick panes of glass.

I continue. "There have been days I've published stuff and didn't think anything else about it. But then when I'd wake up in the morning, in the quiet still just before dawn – during those pre-dawn hours when I believe the Lord speaks to me often in that 'Alpha state' of sleep – and I'd get a bad feeling about something I'd published."

"But why?"

"I don't know, maybe it was too scandalous or not helpful or whatever, but all I know was that it gave me a funny feeling. So I'd end up un-publishing it. I even had a nightmare that Satan smiled at me over one book so I took it off the market and threw the unsold copies away."

"Word?" he asks, surprised, the numbers turning in his head. "How much did that cost you?"

"Nearly 10K," I say.

"I'll bet your husband wasn't happy about that."

"No. But he got over it," I say, ready to finally hit him with the heart of my question for him. "Haven't you ever felt that way about your music? Your lyrics?"

"What? Me? Naw..." Geno says, leaning back in his chair, diverting his eyes, backtracking from the previous admissions he'd made. "I mean, it was just entertainment."

"I get that – but what about the people who were listening to your music, thinking that was your real life?"

"Most of us weren't gang-bangers; those were those hangers on up in the studio," he says, his voice rising higher. "The ones shooting that 12-gauge into the concrete floor were those people who caught the vapors, wanting to be famous by hanging around us. You should have seen the Cell Block studio entrance – it was just like a plain door and that's it up in that fancy building."

"Well, the media coverage of that studio shooting was awesome," I say, trying to keep him on track. "Thank God nobody got hurt..." I pause, realizing what I'm saying awkwardly, "...at least that time."

"Yeah well, the media was attracted to the violence," Geno says, obviously getting irritated. "They were the ones who started calling it 'gangsta rap' in the first place. The media started that whole 'East Coast versus West Coast' mess."

"Hold up," I say, unafraid of him, perhaps because we have been separated this time by the thick glass. "You can't blame everything on the media. We only report what we're told or what we research – at least that's the way it should work." I hold up Dee's journal once more and shake it in the air. "Or at least what we learn from the horse's mouth."

A wave of sadness floats over Geno; his posture slumps down farther in the seat as if someone has doused him with a bucket of slop.

I lower my voice to a softer tone, knowing that my next questions might send him into a deep trance of remembrance or straight back to his cell and me homeward bound. "Why don't you tell me your version of what happened the night Dee was killed? I've read about her suspicions of him cheating in the journal – but obviously, her writing stops at a certain point. Don't let the bloggers and journalists have the final word. Tell us what happened yourself."

Geno exhales louder than I've ever heard. He wipes the palm of his large hand across his face from his forehead downward, across his neck.

"Okay," he relents, even quieter than me, barely above a whisper.

The prison drops away as he talks, and the scenario changes to a place without walls, back when Geno is at the top of his game and only marginally aware of a young rapper named Lucas – who goes by the rap name Lasso – who idolizes and imitates "Big Geno" from afar.

§ § §

A non-descript baby blue-colored home sits high atop a hill in Culver City, a city in the western part of Los Angeles County, California. Inside, the modest looking home opens to a large living room with sleek wooden floors.

Through the sliding glass doors, the vista of the backyard, filled with fruit trees, dips low into a crevice.

In the spacious dining area, Kim paces as she watches Dee dressed in a super short black miniskirt, applying lipstick in heavy loops across her lips as she preens in a large round mirror near the front door.

"Lasso's here," Dee shouts.

"Wait, baby, wait," Kim says to Dee, then begins pulling at a thin black bespectacled man who sits in a chair, engrossed in his magazine. "Will you talk to her, please?"

"I tried," he says, barely glancing up. "She won't listen to me."

"Why should I?" Dee shouts. "He ain't *none* of my daddy!"

A loud car horn sounds from outside.

"I'll be back," Dee says, opening the door slightly. "Oh wait, I forgot my..." She turns and runs back up to her room.

"Forgot what?" Kim asks, looking from Lasso – who sits in a red convertible sports car as it idles – to her husband, a man who does all he can to avert everyone's eyes.

"Forgot what?" she calls out louder to Dee, who is upstairs in her room. Kim turns to her husband. "He doesn't even have the decency to come inside." She peeks out at Lasso, who drums his fingers impatiently on the black steering wheel. His eyes are hidden behind dark, pitch-black sunglasses as he honks the horn harder.

"You know what?" Kim says, stomping toward the door.

"Ma! No!" Dee yells, running down the stairs, carrying a small black bag. "You'll embarrass me."

"Look, he's not going to come to our home and disrespect me," Kim declares. "You are too good for him."

"Ma, he has a top ten hit right now," Dee whines.

"I don't care what he has; Lasso needs to have some manners and respect your family and your home," she says, folding her arms, surveying her daughter up and down. "I'm going to have to talk to Geno about all this."

Dee laughs. "Lots of luck with that one. I'll see y'all later. *Much* later."

"Where are you going?" Kim asks. "You're not staying out all night again, I swear."

"I'm just going to the studio. I'll be back. *Holla!*"

§ § §

Inside the studio, Dee sits back on a couch as Lasso drinks shots with a bunch of men and women. Heavy bass beats permeate the place, with everyone seemingly drunk and high except for Dee, who beams at Lasso as he stands and wobbles.

"And *Imma* throw the peace sign, and *Imma* throw the deuce," Lasso rhymes, freestyle.

"Yeah!" the small crowd bobs their heads.

"*Imma* be that Nigga with Illuminati truth."

"Yo, that's tight," says one of the girls.

"You think I throw my Horus," Lasso whispers, making a circle out of his hands and placing it on his forehead. "You think I throw my sixes, well I'm gon' throw your whore up and let her hit my switches."

"Whoa!"

Dee's smile fades a bit as Lasso grabs one of the women in the group around her waist, and her skinny frame topples in front of him.

§§§

"So Lasso was in the Illuminati?" I ask Geno, snapping us back to the present day. "How long has that been around?"

"Don't ask me," Geno says. "Kim would try and tell me all about it. I thought it was a joke, all a bunch of hooey from my paranoid baby's mama."

"Is it real?"

"I don't even concern myself with it now. All I know was Kim would send me all this data about secret signs and hand signals and shapes and so much stuff. She wanted me to get Dee away from him with the quickness."

"Why did Lasso do all that? I read all this stuff about the triangle signs he'd use and how carefully he'd construct his concerts to have a ring he could move around within," I say.

"Kim would try and warn me about that. She talked about some secret society and how Lasso thought it would give him special powers and make him more popular," Geno says, furrowing his brows.

"What did you do? What did you tell her?"

"Who Kim or Dee?"

"Both," I say, curious to hear his response to such evil charges.

"Ain't nobody had time for that," Geno says, looking embarrassed at another non-response. "My new song had hit, I had just gotten away from my greedy manager and started my own label. Everybody was looking for me to fail. That's why I had to succeed."

"Yeah, you'd been in the rap game for a minute by that time," I recall.

"People thought I was old or something," Geno says, "or that I couldn't survive without BWO and Jeffrey. Like I couldn't just be Geno Cide and hold it down on my own."

"And you did," I nod.

"Yeah I did," Geno shakes his head. "But none of it seems worth it now. None of it."

§ § §

The flashback emerges with such clarity for Geno. He is in the studio, solo in the booth, scribbling on a composition journal when he hears a noise. He stops, reaches for the gun in his jacket then drops it back into the large space when he sees Kim's face.

"Girl, you could've got dropped! Are you crazy bustin' up in here at 2 a.m. unannounced like this?" Geno says, laughing at his own fear.

"It seems like the only time I'll be sure to find you – and the only place I know you'll be when you're in town," she says.

Geno motions to two guys sitting at a huge soundboard to take a five-minute break by throwing his opened palm up at them. Kim is miffed, knowing full well what the wordless communication means.

"So the mother of your child only gets five minutes of the great Geno Cide's time, huh?" she asks.

"Look – you don't mind it when you're cashing my checks, do you? The mortgage is always paid, ain't it?"

"Geno, I didn't come here to argue with you. I'm really worried about Dee – I mean, *for real, for real* this time."

"You're always worried too much about her," he says. "You always have been. But she's growing up now. Before we know it, she'll be married and having babies."

"But not with him!" Kim yells louder than she intends, wiping the goofy grin off of Geno's mouth. "Not with Lasso. She can't marry him."

"What's the big deal? Come on now, I've got to get back to this recording. She ain't getting married."

Kim searches the padding on the walls, touching them, marveling at how they looked so dark, like a deep gray version of egg cartons lining the walls. She looks for a way to express her deep concern to Geno as his impatience grows, and he places his huge headphones on either side of his temples.

"I've always lost out to your music, haven't I? Well, it's something about *this* guy," she says. "I get a weird feeling about him. It's not even that he's a rap star – obviously – but there's this dark side. I can't shake it."

Geno taps Kim hard on her upper arm, as if he's "dapping up" one of his boys. "Don't sweat it, on the real. I can fall through sometime when he's there and holler at him."

Kim purses her lips and twists them to the side, eyeing Geno through eyes that have shifted far to their corners to look at him. "I mean it, Geno, I really need you to talk to her."

"I said I will," he snaps, nodding to his friends at the soundboard, who start a pulsing beat once more that drowns out their voices. "I'll hit you up," Geno yells above the din of the loud beats, pulling his humongous headphones back on his ears, literally spitting as he rhymes with newfound fervor, "Don't F with my MRS!"

Kim quietly leaves the studio as Geno continues to rap:

My Money...

My Rep...

My Sex-ies...

My M.R.S....

My wife...

To protect her, nigga...

I'll take your mofo life

§ § §

"So that's when 'Don't F with my MRS' was created," I say. "Can I be honest? I hate that song."

"A lot of women did," Geno admits. "That's what started all the protests."

"But that's what really put you on the map," I say, raising my hand high above my head. "That horrible song put you on a whole new level. I mean, even white suburban soccer moms knew who you were after that one."

"Yep – don't mess with my money, my respect, or my sex."

"You were serious about that one," I say, thinking back on the lyrics of the song that praised having a high income and the ability to attract women and be feared above all.

"Shoot, after that song, I ain't have to worry about getting on the cover of hip-hop magazines like *The Source* or *XXL* no more," Geno leans back, stretching and smiling at his own accomplishment. "I got *Rolling Stone* and *Fortune*. By myself."

"But it seems so, so *hateful*," I say. "It doesn't seem like you at all. Not like you seem now."

"Everybody had gotten used to that hard image of a gangster rap artist who was, in essence, a pimp," he says. "I had to go over the top. I had to give the fans more of what they wanted from me. I had to go hard or go home – and I wasn't going home."

"That video," I say, remembering the uncut version that I watched recently on YouTube, forcing myself to sit through the images of Geno slashing others, while he stood in a rainstorm of cash and coins.

"I got that idea from reading the newspaper's crime section," he says. "I started reading all these horrible stories about serial killers and the ways they killed people. I put others' words in my mouth and in the first person to sound hard."

"That was a dangerous thing to do," I note.

"How you figure?" Geno asks.

"Well," I pause, unsure if I should tell him. "The image merged with reality."

The guard clears his throat, shifting his position several feet off to the right, standing in the corner. I know my time with Geno is short, and yet I feel we have so much more to cover, to finally get closer to the violence that is at the epicenter of his prison stay.

"You've got to give me more," I say, staring directly into his eyes, hoping Geno will express his deepest feelings and vulnerabilities at last. "You are at the precipice of a big change. Do you realize how the sentiment of your fans is shifting in your favor? It's not smart to let whatever happened keep eating you alive. Tell me about that night. Tell me something."

Geno clutches the black phone until the veins on the back of his hand curve prominently like rapid rivers. He cups his free hand over his mouth as he speaks, an odd move to make when talking to a reporter who is writing your life story.

"A'ight. Here it is," he says, stopping, as if pausing for the most dramatic response. In actuality, I see that Geno is trying to force the words out of his throat beyond the lumps of emotion that threaten to hold them down. "Kim tried to get Dee to break up with Lasso, but he convinced Dee to run away with him instead. I was finally supposed to talk to her that night at the Grammy's, because we would've all been there together – and I would've finally known where she was."

"It was at the Staples Center that year," I say.

"Yup," he says, visible tears starting to streak his face, running from the corner of one eye and diagonally across his nose, dripping on his chin in large volumes, forcing him to catch his breath.

"It's okay, it's okay...it'll be okay."

§ § §

Dee is wearing a cherry-red colored strapless gown that matches the color of Lasso's convertible luxury car as he drives slowly out of a garage in a stunning Hollywood Hills home.

"You are a serious dime piece," Lasso says, stroking her face, taking in the color of her crimson lips and extra made-up face. "You look so mature."

"Are you trying to tell me I look old?" Dee laughs in the gentle warm breeze that sends her shoulder-length, curly hair dancing around her head like a halo as Lasso speeds up.

"You look like you belong with all of us stars."

"And you look like the handsome super star you are," Dee says, flipping the lapel of Lasso's black tuxedo.

The red Ferrari slows to a crawl at a stop light before approaching the Staples Center. Lasso's cell phone rests idly in the drink carrier, sparking to life with a text message. Dee looks down at the face of the phone, which shows a preview of the message prior to cutting off.

"*Let's hook up after?*" Dee repeats. "Who is that from?"

"What?" Lasso asks, grabbing his phone quickly and unplugging it from the car charger. He slides the phone into his inside jacket pocket.

"Who was that, Lasso? Some side chick?"

"It was probably my manager finding out if I could do that post-Grammy interview," he says quickly, stepping on the gas and acting overly interested in streetlights and street signs.

"Let me see it then, if it's so innocent." Dee holds out her palm, sucking her teeth and waiting for him to hand over the phone.

"Naw, girl, stop tripping."

"Why am I tripping? Why can't I see your phone? Let me see your phone, Lasso!"

Dee reaches across his chest and tries to feel for the pocket where he placed the phone. She jabs her hand quickly into the inside of his jacket as she feels the phone within her grasp.

"Are you crazy, girl?" Lasso jerks the wheel with great exaggeration, causing the car to screech and swerve. Other cars honk behind them. "Stop it!"

"Why are you tripping? Why can't I see your phone if everything is so innocent and on the up and up?" Dee screams, tears streaking her face with black mascara running down her cheeks.

"You look crazy! You look like a crazy ass bitch right now!" Lasso screams back.

"You stop! Stop the car right now!" Dee grabs the wheel and tries to steer it all the while using her left hand to dig around in Lasso's clothes. He takes the phone and drops it into a side pocket of the car on the driver's side. She takes off her seat belt and lurches farther across his lap, trying to retrieve the smartphone out of the car's pocket.

"Get out. Get the hell out, right now," Lasso says, suddenly strangely calmer.

"Oh, you gonna kick me out your car now? In the middle of the street?" Dee cries. "Again? Tonight of all nights?"

Lasso reaches across her to open her side of the door, wrestling and pushing until he sends Dee falling onto the gravel on the side of the road. She instinctively puts her hands out in front of herself to catch her fall as she lands hard. Immediately, she turns her hands over and sees streaks of blood streaming out of fresh cuts made by the rocks.

"Look what you did, Lasso! Don't you dare leave me out here," she screams, drawing the attention of a line of cars that pass by. Dee lifts herself to a standing position and then begins to wave at passing cars.

Confused drivers begin to slow down and wonder what the melee is about. Lasso becomes enraged at Dee and the way she is trying to get help by beckoning to onlookers.

Lasso jumps out and starts pulling Dee back toward his car.

"Oh so now you want me back?" Dee pulls away from his clenched grip around her arm. "I'm going to tell everybody what you did!" Dee runs over to a white car that has stopped to watch them, the male driver confused over whether to exit his car or not. She waves her bleeding hands in his direction.

"Get back in this car, girl!" Lasso picks her up by her waist and body slams her into the passenger side of the car, lifting her up and over the opened convertible rooftop.

Dee lands hard as Lasso jumps over the other side and burns rubber as he speeds away from the scene. "Don't ever test me!"

He punches the side of her face so hard while he's driving that he can barely keep the car on the winding road. Dee's head wobbles, taking the blows.

"Stop it, Lasso! Stop…" she breathes out a whisper, her breath trying to recover. "It's me, Lasso. Stop."

After some time, Lasso stops the car at a point overlooking the brilliant lights of Los Angeles. The ugliness of the violent event stands in sharp contrast to the gorgeous high point at an observatory overlook across from the Hollywood sign.

Dee is still afraid of him, but he is moving into the apologetic honeymoon phase. "I'm so sorry baby, I'm so sorry," he says. "I didn't mean it. I don't know what happened. It's like I blacked out with anger or something."

"I need some air," Dee huffs as she weakly opens her door and stumbles out. Lasso follows her as she wanders around.

"Come on back, you can't be out her alone," he says, all of a sudden a caring and different kind of man. "They have mountain lions out here."

"I'd probably be safer," Dee says. She returns to his car and they sit. "How could you do all this to me? Why would you treat me so badly?"

"I would never cheat on you baby," Lasso says, rubbing her hair. "I'd rather kill myself than hurt you, Dee."

He reaches down in the middle section of his car and takes out an old-fashioned revolver and begins twirling the cylinder randomly, putting it to his own head intermittently.

"Lasso, don't do that," Dee says, one hand on her door, ready to exit the car again. "Take me home."

"Would you miss me?" he asks, spinning it again and pulling the trigger.

Dee screams. Nothing happens.

Lasso laughs. "Don't trip. It's not loaded." He spins it again, puts the nozzle in his mouth and pulls the trigger once more. Nothing.

"How do you know it's empty?" Dee says, still shaking.

"I checked," he says, flipping the cylinder open, spinning it and peering through the holes in the darkness. He closes the cylinder once more, points it straight at her forehead until it touches her skin.

Dee closes her eyes, but doesn't scream. She is stoic, stock-still and relenting, as if she knows what's going to happen.

"It's *empty*," Lasso says, laughing. "See?" he asks, pulling the trigger back once more. Instead of the quiet click of another empty round, the gun blasts a bullet that flashes out of the nozzle with a streak of fire, causing Dee's head to jerk back.

Blood, brains and bone fragments land everywhere. Lasso is beyond shock. He drops the gun and screams her name over and over again.

§ § §

"I'm so sorry, Geno," I say. "I don't know what else to say."

A certain blank stare comes across his face, and Geno is quiet for a long time. I let the space remain silent, hoping that he'll continue, and dig into the rest of the events of that pivotal evening before they disappear like so much mist in his private memories.

"That's what was in the police report," Geno says. "That's what Lasso told police he did to my sweet baby girl."

"They must've taken his statement while still at the scene then..." I say, trailing off, wishing and compelling him to finish my thoughts.

"Yeah, they had him up in the hills for a long time," Geno says. "He was still there right after I found out. I could tell people were acting weird at the Grammys."

A faraway look comes across his face again. He is pensive. Finally, he speaks.

"They say most people get bit by snakes when trying to examine them closer. Run away from snakes," he advises. "Or kill them."

§ § §

Geno is stunting and posing, smiling for the red carpet cameras before he enters the awards ceremony with his entourage. He struts inside, immediately picking up on the palpable reaction of the stars and their managers around the venue.

"What's up with all the whispering, man?" Geno asks one of the guys in his crew. The guy shrugs.

More groups of people walk by, pointing at him and speaking lowly to one another.

"What?" Geno asks once more. He reaches in his jacket and sees many missed calls, voice mails and texts. "What is going on tonight, dude? What is happening?"

Jeffrey spots Geno from across the room and makes a beeline for him, his face stern and serious.

§ § §

"So that's how you found out?" I ask.

"Yep. I knew that if Jeffrey was coming to talk to me like that, looking all serious – talking to me at all – I knew something was really wrong."

"I don't even want to imagine how you felt at that moment," I say. "Finding out your daughter was dead."

"Alexa, it's like I couldn't think straight – all I could think about was Dee being helpless, needing me, getting hurt – and I wasn't there to protect her," he says. "I thought I'd have forever to protect her, to make it up to her for me being gone so many years."

"You never expect to bury your child," I offer.

"Not when they're barely 20."

"Or 23. Not never. You think you have forever."

§§§

Lasso sobs in the back of a police car, his hands cuffed behind his back. He is sideways on the seat, screaming and halfway out of his mind with worry and grief.

Geno and his crew pull up nearby the bevy of police, who have the area blocked off with yellow crime tape. An ambulance pulls away from the scene, its lights eerily flashing red but with no siren sounding. It drives off at normal speed.

"Are you the father?" a police officer asks Geno, carefully steering him away from the cop car where Lasso still lays, hollering and kicking at the doors.

Geno pretends to be calm. "Yes, officer, yes I am. Can I ask what happened?" he says, keeping his eye on the car where Lasso is writhing around inside.

A volcano of emotion is seething and bubbling beneath Geno's forced exterior as he speaks in a monotone manner with the policeman, nodding and pretending he is taking in his answers.

As soon as the officer takes his eyes off Geno, he runs straight for the car where Lasso is and pulls out a gun from his waistband. He empties all the rounds into the back seat where Lasso lays. Lasso is hit and grows silent. No more kicking in the car.

"Drop your weapon!" the officer commands Geno, who drops the gun on the ground, lifts his hands in the sky and kicks the gun away from him.

§§§

"I'm just amazed that you're here on death row," I say. "I know a man lost his life – but what about crimes of passion or self defense or something? He killed your daughter!"

"Yeah, I know people who did worse who haven't been sitting on death row for years like me," he says. "Besides, the president at the time I was convicted was big on the war on crime, so I was the perfect popular patsy to make an example out of."

"I believe it," I say. "I don't know a lot about the law, but I just got called for jury duty last month and these women were sitting there in the waiting room talking about, 'Hang 'em, let him fry!' They didn't even know the guys on trial. They were judging them and calling them ruthless criminals."

"Yeah, people don't realize what a slippery slope life can be," he says. "All of a sudden the gangster rapper that I rapped about, that I pretended to be, became me."

§ § §

There it was.

Geno had finally unveiled his soul and told another living soul about that night's events that led to his incarceration. The man who'd refused all other interviews and didn't even testify during his own trial had at last opened up and agreed to tell the tragic story about his rise to fame and fall from grace.

Part of me was relieved to know Geno's journey, but now that I did, another feeling was taking over, all the way on the drive home from San Quentin until I lay down to try and sleep. There must be a reason that he is opening up. He must want to be free – or at least, a stay of execution to live the rest of his life in prison.

I turn over in bed, sliding the brightness of my tablet down to the dimmest setting in order to not wake my husband, then promptly Google things like "death row San Quentin," choosing one YouTube video after another about the topic.

"Inmates sit on death row while we spend millions and millions of dollars," says one woman in the videos, and I marvel at how many of the videos I discover are ones that seem to be against capital punishment – if not for the morality of it, but for the high cost of the process.

"California houses 22% of all death row inmates in the country," I learn, thinking of how the statistics are no longer numbers, but within each one there is Geno's face and his predicament. Although he hasn't voiced it yet, within his actions of telling his testimony seems the apparent desire to keep living.

As numbers flash before my tablet and my brain, like the $134 million over and above that's spent on death row inmates as opposed to those who get life without a possibility of parole, the next purpose for my articles for Geno spring to life.

"Wait a minute…is this legal?" I ask myself aloud, thinking of Geno asleep in that single cell as I enjoy the luxury of my king sized bed. "The average time on death row in California is 30 years. A lot of executions would have to take place before Geno's turn," I whisper quietly.

With every new webpage discovered, like how one innocent man who was eventually exonerated in Texas had been on death row for more than 20 years – or the fact that California has had no executions since 2006, and seems to have a growing sympathy toward getting rid of the death penalty altogether – getting Geno a stay of execution starts to seem more like a reality than a fantasy or false notion hiding in the back of his mind that he won't speak out loud...yet.

The next visit to see Geno must have good news – and I want to bring it to him. It seems he's owed something, that man who has just begun to understand the error of his ways – seemingly too late to make a change. But there's got to be something that society can give a man who was avenging the death of his own daughter. Or more rightly, something Geno can give them to make up for the years of destruction and violence he caused by spreading all those hateful, violent lyrics that seemed to come home to roost in a major way in his own family.

"For such a time as this," Geno had said earlier this evening during a break in the heavy conversation.

Those words now resonate in my mind as I fall asleep. "For such a time as this," I repeat, knowing exactly the next move to get Geno more of the positive press he deserves, at least if he's willing to continue to admit to the hate he spewed through his rap in the first place that somehow caused this whole life chain of events to occur.

Chapter 5:

Money Ain't a Thang

It's a collect call from Geno at San Quentin. I know it before I even look at my cell phone, almost by the sound of the ringtone, even though Geno doesn't have a special ringtone on my phone. It's like when people who are so in tuned with one another pick up the phone at the same time – so soon after the other one dials that the receiving party's phone doesn't even have a chance to ring.

"I heard you thinking about me," I say to Geno, something my mom used to say to me. I tell him this quickly, as soon as I accept the charges – before the same "*blah blah blah, you-are-on-the-phone-with-a-San-Quentin-prisoner*" recorded reminder that I've grown accustomed to during these exactly 15-minute long calls has a chance to jump in and annoyingly interrupt our conversation.

"Why's that?" he asks, cutting quickly to the chase, understanding the fast tempo urgency of our words. Geno is displaying the lightning speed wit that made his flow famous worldwide.

"*Rolling Stone* bought an excerpt of our book," I tell him. "They're going to publish a 7-page spread – in both their print and online editions – and they're going to put you on the cover."

"Well isn't this full circle," he says, pleasantly and reflectively. "The cover of the *Rolling Stone* once again. Good – hopefully they're paying you enough to take care of all these collect calls."

"Don't worry about it, they are," I say, shifting onto my left side to stare out over the hills, still burnt the golden brown color that allegedly gave the Golden State its nickname. The winter rains have not yet come to turn them a deep lush green.

"When do they want it?"

"I want to get it to them right away – to keep this ball rolling while the momentum over your case is growing," I pause, quickly grabbing a small notebook with a cold gold cover decorated with a fleur-de-lis symbol on the top and a pen. "Let's make this opportunity count and give them even more of a reason to see you as a full person – you know, the full measure of the man. HuffPo wants a short piece, too."

"HuffPo?"

"*The Huffington Post*," I explain, once again forgetting that 21st century things that are so common to us on the outside – like smartphones, solar panels, tablets, popular websites and gaming consoles – can seem like inventions from *The Jetsons* to the men and women who've been locked up for years on end without much (if any) access to them. "It's a huge website that covers everything from the political to the personal celebrity pieces. People call it *HuffPo* for short."

"Oh snap! All right then. *School me.* Shoot," he prompts. "I'm all ears. And mouth. For answers, that is."

"Okay, here's what I've been thinking: We hardly know anything about your mother or father," I say, trying to balance the need to move speedily and with brevity against the sensitive stance that Geno's ego requires. "I thought for *Rolling Stone* we could flesh out what we have so far, and really make it intense and more thought-provoking by examining your childhood."

I wait for a reply through the breathing. Almost as if saved by the bell, the recording breaks the flow, giving Geno the perfect excuse to switch tactics.

"Naw..." he says, "you can just keep going like we've been going."

He's clamming up again, I see.

"Geno, I appreciate the creative freedom you've given me," I plead softly, "but people are going to want to know the things that have driven you to do what you've done. They need to know your back-story – your real back-story."

"I've already told people my history," he says. "You can look it up."

"I've tried," I proclaim. "It's not much there."

More silence. In the space of me waiting, listening to his breathing, almost literally seeing the wheels in the sky keep on turning as if he's debating whether to open up one more door to his soul to this probing reporter – and not merely any door, like the private bedroom door he opened previously, admitting to Lasso's killing, but a faraway basement door that's been shut so long it has warped with age, and is covered in dirty cobwebs and the carcasses of dead centipedes – I think of the research into his history I performed.

"Even the microfiche articles I found at the library don't offer much about your parents," I explain, recounting the exhaustive research I've performed into Geno's life. Indeed, this seems to be the sticking point and locale where the former rap star has shut out every other journalist who has crept near that door, frighteningly and bravely prepared to spray away the spider webs and pry open the curved wooden door with a crowbar, if need be, to get to the long held secrets within.

"People just want to be nosey," he says, growing loud – trying to "loud-talk me" (another mother aphorism) – and leaving our soft and sensitive tones far behind.

"What I want to know is what made you write lines like, 'Put her butt in the trunk and say sayonara to that ass,' or even worse. Stuff I don't even want to repeat," I say. "I need to know your deeper motivation. Where did it come from? Why do you hate women?"

"I don't hate women. I love women," Geno claims, and I can hear him smiling through the phone, turning on that well-practiced charm that tries to dissuade and throw people off the red-hot scent they've found on a track or trail like a bloodhound.

"Love and lust are not the same thing, even though people confuse them," I say, not allowing him to move me with charisma. "When my husband walked in the bitter cold around 2 a.m. to get me medicine from the store, that's love. What Jesus did on the cross? That's ultimate love. When a man throws out lines like, 'Baby let me bone you, you're so banging,' but then tosses her to the curb when his wife finds out – that's lust."

"I get it," Geno says, "but I don't know what you want me to tell you."

I sit up, pen poised above the small square of paper, getting ready for an earful about his formative years.

"All right," I begin, "why don't you start talking about your mother? What was it like being raised by a single mother who didn't have a whole lot of help?"

"I don't talk about my mother," he says solidly. "There's no reason to bring her into this now. We don't really speak. We don't really get down like that – you know, like a normal mother and son."

"Why not?" I ask. "Was it her you were talking about in that 'Poison Box' song? Was she promiscuous or something?"

"Hey, hey, hold up now—" Geno starts talking, but is interrupted by a sudden rumbling that comes both from his end and mine simultaneously, as I watch the closed glass doors rattle against their door frames.

"Do you feel that?" I ask him, afraid.

"Yeah," he says, putting on a brave cadence for me. "It's all right, it ain't that bad. You know we Californians don't get out of bed for anything less than a 4.0 quake."

We laugh nervously together. "This is definitely more than a 4.0," I say, standing up, walking around my bedroom, marveling at how the normally dormant ceiling fan's chain begins swaying, as if in the center of a windstorm.

"It's a rolling one," he says, "not like the kind that bang up and down."

"Probably 5.7 or more," I guesstimate. "I wonder where the epicenter is located."

"Gotta be in between us if we both felt it. Maybe north of San Rafael or somewhere."

The earth calms, but I stand, still guarded. "It's over. Now we've just got to watch out for aftershocks."

"True, true," he says.

"All right, let's get back on topic before we get cut off," I say, and all of a sudden I realize my voice is bouncing back at me, and I'm speaking to a dead line.

How convenient, once more. If I didn't know any better, I would think Geno took it upon himself to hang up on me and disappear – instead of waiting for the prison's phone call system to automatically disconnect the call when 15 exact minutes had elapsed.

How could Geno do this? Doesn't he understand how much it would help him and help the book to disclose the experiences that really drove him to write such hateful lyrics? Fine, if he wants to leave me twisting in the wind like this, I'll go and write the most fascinating portrait I can – without more of his assistance.

§ § §

Pastor Prince has come with me, like some sort of blessed reinforcement that part of me knows I'll need during this visit to the prison. Even the ominous gray clouds hanging over the mountain in the distance bespeak something unpleasant to come.

"Geno should be excited once he sees all the rallies that have been organized all over the country since that *Rolling Stone* article came out," Pastor Prince says, grinning as we walk from our respective cars towards the prison.

"I hope so. He made it as a trending topic on Twitter and everything," I say. "People even set up flash mob events and recorded them and put them on YouTube to bring more attention to Geno."

"Well, what did he say?" he asks me excitedly, his mouth open in a genuine smile that matches his anticipation.

"I don't know," I answer. "Nothing. I mailed Geno the article two weeks ago. He hasn't called me or anything."

"Oh...that's weird," Pastor Prince says.

"Quite peculiar," I concur, "I mean, seeing as though we usually talk and visit so often. For the book, that is."

The pastor furrows his brows curiously at me, but then turns his querying gaze toward the prison, as if he's trying to look through the walls straight into the face of the man he's known for more than half of his lifetime, trying to cut to the marrow of the situation.

"I'm so glad you came with me," I say.

"Me too."

Geno is upset. This is apparent even within the spacious walls of the interview room afforded us by the prison, where we meet with Geno and an ever-present guard. It should be a joyously momentous occasion, considering all the progress that has been made since we last met, but Geno is not happy.

The man of God's "Spidey senses" pick it up, too.

"What's up, man?" Pastor Prince asks Geno. "What's up with you?"

The men greet one another, but Geno can't help but blurt out what he's really thinking upon first laying eyes on me. "You think I'm responsible for my daughter's death! You think Lasso killed her ultimately because of me!"

I'm not taking this venom, I think to myself, glancing from the guard back to Geno, wondering how "crunk" we're allowed to get up in this piece. "That's not what I said, that's what you said. I was just quoting and paraphrasing and expounding upon the points you made."

Pastor Prince holds out his arms wide, keeping the space wide between us like a referee holding two opponents back to their corners who are chomping at the bit for the bell to ring so they can dance again in the boxing ring. The guard snaps to the ready, at attention, as if he could drag Geno back to his cell at any moment.

"Chill man, chill," Pastor Prince urges, giving Geno a stern look that transcends any roles of "man of the cloth" versus "superstar felon rapper" that they may exist within now. No, this is the glare from one road dog to another, from one "home slice" telling the other "home skillet" to hold it down.

Miraculously, something about the way the pastor approaches his old friend works to calm Geno down. He sits, less angry but still serious. "It's not my fault what Lasso did to Dee. Just because he listened to me all those years...you made it seem like I gave him some kind of blueprint straight to my daughter."

I shake my head. "That's not what I was trying to get across. I was trying to express the effects of your writing."

"They were just lyrics. Just words. I ain't nobody's role model."

A soft answer turns away wrath, I repeat to myself before responding.

"Whether you are willing to accept it or not, you were quite the big role model. Kids looked up to you. They know your lyrics by heart to this day. They thought the things you said were real."

Geno puts his head in his hands.

"Listen to her, man," Pastor Prince says. "It's the same stuff I used to tell you and you weren't trying to hear it then, either."

"When you said stuff like 'smack that trick' that's exactly what they did," I say, surprised at how readily I recall Geno's memorized lyrics from a full two decades ago. "When you talked about your pimp stick, they went out and got one and used it."

"The proverbial pimp stick," Pastor Prince says, without rhyme or reason , as if it means more to him and Geno than I even have been made privy to know.

"I won't take that on me," Geno pipes up. "I won't accept that. That's on their own parents to raise them."

"Some of them didn't have any parents – no parents who cared – so they turned to you," Pastor Prince interjects. "And even some of the ones who did have parents, those parents were too busy with their careers or didn't give two flips about what was really going on in their own households."

Geno knows the words are an unveiled reference to him. "Hey man, not everybody grew up with no 'Brady Bunch' type of upbringing, man. Not everybody had 'The Cosby Show' in their own house and grew up to be pastors." He pauses, as if choking back tears. "Some of us had to do what we had to do to get it poppin'."

"I got it, dude," Pastor Prince says, reaching out to slightly tap the top of Geno's hand. "You know I know what you went through, brauh."

My eyes light up, wondering if I can tap him as a resource to figure out the big mystery that is Geno's childhood.

"Now you need to get it more," he says, causing Geno to squint his gaze, and twist his mouth, as if he's on the verge of giving in to an admission. "You've already accepted the murder charge. Now you must accept the consequences of what your words have wrought on this nation – on a whole generation."

Geno is rocking his noggin back and forth, but the fact that this master lyricist remains silent as he listens intently shows that he is indeed taking the constructive criticism into his being, letting it flip and turn over in the space behind his sternum and within his heart.

"Sometimes the chickens do come home to roost," Pastor Prince says quietly. "But we can go ahead and take the same chickens and the mess that we've made and make good meat out of them that ministers to others and ourselves."

Finally we shut our mouths, both knowing that the other is praying similarly as fervently for some kind of big breakthrough as Geno at last parts his lips and lets sound come out.

"You made me look like a womanizer," he finally says in my general direction, and I can see the straightened and hopeful posture of both Pastor Prince and I dip at the same time, in deflated slumps.

You are a womanizer, I think to myself, along with a word that's very un-Christ-like that rhymes with "sucker" that my convictions tell me not to say or write. I do not speak these words out loud because I know the ultimate goal is to get this project done and done quickly if we want to have any kind of impact upon his upcoming death date.

"I want to pull the book," Geno announces when it nears the time for our visit to end.

He wants to pull the book? Is he kidding?

"Geno, this book can *help* you," Pastor Prince says, exasperated. The way he says "help" with such intonation and fervor, it reminds me of that scene in *Jerry Maguire* wherein Tom Cruise's character implores Cuba Gooding, Jr.'s thick-headed and stubborn football-playing Rod Tidwell to *"help me help you"* over and over again, slower still – breaking at various points in the phrase to get the man to listen to reason.

Help…me…help…you, Geno. I want to beg. *Gennooooooo!*

Whoever his mother was or is, she surely named him correctly with that "no" tacked on the end of his name. I can't believe it, all this hard work and time and hours spent tossing over what to write, how to present him in a palatable way to the public that goes up against the types of lyrics that he has spewed out. How dare he?

"I'm on your side," I remind him. "It's true: I am hoping and praying God gives me the words that transition this tide of public sympathy towards you to the point where your death sentence is repealed. Don't you get it? Don't you hope? Don't you understand?"

"Believe me, Ma," he says. "I get it more than you do."

I find it kind of charming that Geno uses an expression reserved for men generally younger than him to say, like the young bucks who ask women they're interested in things such as, "Hey Mommy, what it do?"

But I am not impressed. "I'm not just some chick here for the hell of it," I tell him, growing angry at his obtuseness. "I am on your side. I am painting a positive portrait of you. Just wait until the real reporters get ahold of you again. They'll show you no mercy."

"They've already done that," Geno says.

I stand up and point at him as I walk away. "So you already know then. You should be glad I'm here and get down on your knees every night and thank God above that he sent me."

Geno looks over to Pastor Prince, who gives him an "I told you so" sort of vibe.

"It is hard for you to kick against the goads," Geno says at last. "That's what I kept hearing God telling me the past couple of days. Okay, let's finish this book and get it published ASAP. I want to go forward."

Exhaling with glee, I feel a huge wave of peace come over the room, as if a big shot of Valium has come down from heaven. The tension is broken and we have once again sandblasted our way through the next onion peel of a layer covering Geno's many-layered emotions.

Pastor Prince stands, gripping Geno's hand as we approach the door.

"This means we need to talk about your parents the next time I visit," I say.

"I'll be ready," Geno says.

"Good," I say. "Thank you."

"All right, man, we'll get back," Pastor Prince says to him – and then, turning to me, he asks, "Are you busy? I've got someplace I want to show you."

"I'm free as a bird," I blurt out, and then realize the magnitude of what I've said as soon as I hear Geno being shuffled back to his cell, the sound of heavy chains following him.

§ § §

"What is this place?" I ask Pastor Prince, who has transported me to a huge warehouse-looking location that's a gray, non-descript building he has just opened the glass doors of using a key from his pocket, and has taken me into a room with a large mahogany wood desk in the center.

"A word from the Lord, I believe," he says, flipping on the light. "Consider it Command Central for our new committee."

"What committee?"

"The Committee to Get Geno Out of Prison," he quips, joking in that way that people do when they get uncomfortable over deadly serious topics. "You think that's too long to put on bumper stickers and our letterhead?"

I laugh back, unsure. "That's funny – but what is this place?"

"Alexa, all this time I've been praying to God to expand my church, and for years now I felt like He was telling me to come up to the San Francisco Bay area – but I kept fighting Him, wondering how in the world I could pull off running a satellite location up here and the church down in L.A."

"Yes, I've seen some pastors install campus pastors – or others get private jets to fly back and forth to services," I say.

"I know, and I didn't want to do that at first because you know how people start calling us 'pimp preachers' and bad names, so I didn't do anything," he says.

"I don't blame you," I say, touching the tops of the tall leather swivel chairs that encircle the long table, still wondering why I am in this conference room.

"Well anyway, God kept opening doors for this offshoot church to open. First He brought this star athlete out of nowhere that offered me access to his private plane, and then came this real estate developer who said he had this building he would let us lease on the cheap…"

"For real?" I ask, incredulously peeking through the window past the large parking lot at the lease sign still near the building's large road sign address.

"Amazing, right? So many things started to fall in line, I knew I was meant to spend more time up here, but I didn't know why – not until today. I mean, that talk with Geno really solidified what I've been feeling in my spirit for a long time now."

"What?" I say, leaning forward as if on the edge of my seat, waiting for the big plot twist in a highly anticipated movie or "the big reveal" in a reality TV weight-loss or home construction show.

"I believe Geno is meant to walk free out of that prison," Pastor Prince says. "God laid it on my heart."

"I hope that's true," I say, smiling. "It feels good to hear you say that out loud. I've been thinking the same thing, but I've been wondering if it's only me that wants him out, or if it's our Creator who really wants to set Geno free."

"Well," Pastor Prince slams the table, "we will soon find out. Since we're getting closer to the execution date – and now there's all this amazing attention on Geno again, I figured we could use this location for a place to meet with people and, you know, corral like-minded souls to help him."

"That's perfect!" I almost shout, tempering my excitement. "I've been researching capital punishment in Canada versus the United States and especially all the changes in California lately with the nation's view shifting against the death penalty."

I begin pacing in one direction as Pastor Prince paces in the opposite direction.

"This is good, this is good," he says, his thought process moving his feet forward. "Maybe we could get that 'Don't Kill for Me' petition revived."

"And I could start a Change.org petition – people love those!"

"We can appeal to the community and all these former fans of Geno's to help," Pastor Prince says, smiling. "Especially a lot of those rappers who were coming up around the same time as Geno – you know, lend some big names to this cause."

"Okay. Plus, I've got tons of emails and comments from readers asking what they could do to help. They could funnel all that energy into something great."

"It's settled. Let's get it started, my sista."

§ § §

The same austere and stark conference room has transformed into an alive and buzzing location with individuals segregated, off completing the specific tasks they've been given for the three-hour shift they're fulfilling at the moment.

A group of five people have their backs turned to me, working the phone lines with standard scripts that trail off into unrehearsed conversations that might find one caller praying for a mother whose son is also in jail, or another giving information about the church service hours. Throughout the thread of the calls is always some kind of talk about Geno and his death penalty sentence, whether the person on the other end of the line finds it fair or not.

"Tell me what you think of this design, Swag," I call out, beckoning to a fair-skinned younger woman with tattoos all over her arms, body art that is readily displayed and unfettered by the white wife beater tank top she wears.

She is Swag-a-tarrius, a lesbian rapper who threw me for a loop when she contacted our group, wanting to be part of the movement to help the fellow hip-hop artist she considers a mentor.

"A'i'ght, let me check it out," she says with an exaggerated Puerto Rican accent that is not her own. The silver loop of a lip ring that graces her bottom lip highlights her femininity and the hot pink lipstick she sports today.

I lean to the right, allowing her to view the latest design I've mocked up on the TeeSpring.com website that I've navigated to on my MacBook Air, allowing her to get an uninterrupted vista of my screen, which shows T-shirts with "Free Geno Cide" splayed in a bright yellow font across the front.

"That's straight, real nice," she says, staring at the design. "What if you change the black to purple?"

"You think that'd look better?" I ask, and click on the purple color from a short list of other colors. The shirt color immediately turns a royal-looking color.

"There you go," she says.

"You're right; that looks even better than the black."

"Can you do hoodies, too? You know people love hoodies."

"I'll email them and ask them to do a hoodie, too," I say, clicking a button to save the campaign. "Okay, now the shirts are for sale. We can share this link to all our social media groups: the Facebook fan page, our Twitter feed, Instagram..."

"And I can shoot an email to the Change.org petition signers," Swag says.

"Oh, that's right; I almost forgot about them. They're 50,000 strong and counting every day now," I say.

"Think about all these people walking around in their 'Free Geno Cide' T-shirts, and all the ones who don't know what it means soon will."

"I hope so," I say, glancing at the screen, which reads: "0 out of 50 bought so far" but soon clicks to "1 out of 50 bought so far," causing us to squeal.

"Oh my goodness," she laughs. "Two seconds after you put it up somebody bought one. That's a good sign."

"Yeah it is. This campaign should tip soon and get a lot more sales – all over the world. Hopefully that should at least force them to look at this more like a crime of passion or something."

"From your mouth to God's ear," Swag says.

"It could happen – look what else I found," I say, opening a new tab and navigating through my history to pop up a website I'd previously visited during my research. "Look at all these prisoners that they've set free in California after Prop 36 passed."

She peers over my shoulder into the text of the website article, taking several moments to pause and literally read the piece, not give it the kind of short shrift I've seen others do when surfing online, whereby they read headlines and perhaps subtitles and then assume they know what the entire article is about.

"That's cool but this is about that third strike law," she says. "They got out if the third crime they committed wasn't violent or serious. Geno shot and killed a man."

"Yeah, but it was a man who killed his daughter – doesn't that count for something?" I ask, pleading with her as if she is a convicting jury or something.

"It does in my eyes, but as for the general public? That might only go over if Geno had been right there with them when Lasso was hurting Dee. Then he could've claimed he was directly protecting her."

"I know…" I say, clucking my teeth and scrolling and searching – looking for something, anything…that could be used as a means to help Geno get off death row and see the light of day once more. "But can't they relate? Can't they imagine how they would react if some dude killed their daughters?"

Swag stands up, her biceps naturally flexing as she points to her own breastbone, making the cartoon character cast of angels, dragons and Roman numerals lining her arms dance to life.

"For me, yes, I totally would take somebody out if they hurt my child – and I don't even have any children yet!" she exclaims, breaking through the sadness that our research has brought. "To tell you the truth, though, all some people know about Geno is that he's this hard, has-been gangsta rapper from back in the day who got locked up for popping a younger rapper."

"Yeah, that's what some Midwesterners have told me: the ones who didn't really grow up with rap, or didn't really care about him as a person," I say.

"That's the difference. You've met Geno; you've heard his story. He's a human being to you. There's a certain segment of society who simply views him as another one of those hip-hop heads who got violent and now he's about to be put to death. Good riddance, they say."

"But that's not the whole story," I plead. "Geno is *a man*. He was a father. He's somebody's *son*."

"And that's the side of him that you need to show the world," Swag says, pointing her index finger skyward for emphasis. "That's the missing puzzle piece."

I survey the room, piled high with the paraphernalia that makes it look like the campaign office of someone running for mayor: volunteers, picket signs, good intentions.

"How could I forget?" I ask the woman who can't possibly answer my question. "That's exactly what I've been trying to get from Geno – and the same thing that he said he'd be ready to give me on our next visit. It's like I've been so busy with organizing all these rallies and protests and petitions."

"Like you forgot the main mission," she says.

I stare into her eyes, straight through her, way past this room and into the place I know I must visit next.

§ § §

"I ain't tryin' to look soft," Geno says as soon as I sit down in front of him, my mind ready and willing to take in his words from way back, as he evokes images from his troubled youth growing up in South Central.

"You won't look soft," I say, "you'll look more human."

"How do you know?" he asks, bringing back his common stalling technique that I've learned to work around.

"Because everyone has sympathy for a child, a little boy, especially a hurting little boy," I venture, going with my gut on what to say to keep him talking.

He breathes out hard.

"Imagine I'm not even here," I say through the black phone. "Don't even look at me. Think about it as if you're talking out loud to yourself in your cell."

"I rarely talk out loud to myself in my cell."

"Well, do whatever you have to do," I say, when a light bulb of an idea hits me. "I know! Let's both close our eyes. You talk. I'll listen. And we promise each other no judgments."

"That'll work," Geno says, as if he's encountered the grace from above that he's been seeking all along.

"Good. Start with your mom and dad, and move on from there. Tell me about their marriage," I say.

"We were all good at first," Geno says, talking softly yet confidently, as if these are words he's been waiting eons to divulge. "Believe it or not, my dad was a doctor."

"A *doctor* doctor?" I ask, forcing myself to keep my eyes closed through the surprise. "A medical doctor?"

"Yes, a real live doctor. We actually lived up in Baldwin Hills in the beginning."

"The Black Beverly Hills," I say, knowingly. I can tell we are both smiling, but deep inside, I know Geno still has his eyes shut tight, as do I.

"Yup. I loved it. Had my little friends and sports and stuff," he laughs. "Get this: I even played Lacrosse for a minute."

"Wow, I don't think I know many black people who've played Lacrosse."

"It's an expensive sport," he says. "Anyway, my parents were married and everything, happy – or so I thought. Then they started arguing about Daddy never being home because he was working all those double shifts."

"That had to be hard on your mother."

"I guess, but he was out there working hard, bringing home the bacon. She didn't have to do what she did…" Geno drifts off into silence.

"What did she do?" I ask the reddish-black stillness.

"My mom started bitching at Daddy – I mean, complaining all the time—"

"No judgment, remember? It's okay, just say what you need to say," I encourage him. "We can edit out whatever you'd like later."

"Okay. Well, I was young – like 6 or 7 – but I still remember how they used to fight so much. She would be cool and calm and straight one minute, taking me out to

Baskin Robbins 31 Flavors to get ice cream, taking care of the house and playing happy little homemaker then – boom! – she'd flip the script and start ranting and raving at my father about having put up with all his time away during med school, and how she wasn't going to do it the rest of her life after he became a doctor."

"That had to be hard for her and scary for you," I observe. "I hated it when my parents fought."

"I didn't like it; I was so young I felt like I couldn't do nothing but listen," he says, heaving a heavy sigh – but not of relief. It's one of those sounds that a person makes when they are preparing to lay their souls bare in a way they may have never done before in life to anyone else, anytime else.

"Tell me about their worst fight."

"Well, that's easy. That was the one that led to the divorce," he says succinctly.

"It must've been a bad one."

"It was the worse I'd ever seen – but I knew it was coming," Geno says.

"How could you know?" I ask. "And how old were you by then?"

"I was still a young buck, green and wet behind the ears. Let me think; I had to be only around 8 or 9 by then," he says. "And I knew it was coming, because my mother had started tripping."

"How so?"

"She pretty much stopped all the fussing with Daddy, and I knew why. My mother had started her own little secretarial service, so sometimes she'd take me with her to work – but it wasn't all work. There was some monkey business up in there, too."

I hear Geno shifting around nervously and uncomfortably, but I dare not move nor open my eyes for fear he'll pull away again.

"I remember this one dude had this sweet Mark V car that I sat in the back of, and she told me he was one of her clients that needed some typing job done," Geno reminisces. "So I didn't think nothing of it; I was concentrating and tripping on the car. Even Daddy's car didn't look that good on the inside, with all that plush interior and that kind of diamond shaped window in the back."

"Who was he?" I ask, trying not to sound as interested by his life story as someone watching the latest Spanish telenovela dramatic series unfolding right before their very closed eyes.

"Turns out he was her boyfriend, some guy she met through her same business that Daddy bought for her so she wouldn't be bored," he says.

"That's sad."

"Yeah, I couldn't believe her. Stank trick. Here my father was doing all this stuff for her and she thanks him by screwing some random dude all up in our house – a home that he paid the mortgage on, by the way."

"It's wrong, Geno, I get it. But did you ever think that your mom was just super lonely?" I ask. "Sure, she shouldn't have cheated, but can't you see her position for one minute? I mean, money ain't everything. It can't keep you warm at night."

"Well she should have left him before doing that. Maybe then she wouldn't have got her ass beat," he says.

"By who?"

"By my father. He wasn't a violent man, I promise you. He just got pushed to the edge."

"Oh no – he found out about the cheating?"

"Yeah, my dad came home early one night," Geno says, starting to speak lowly. "He'd told my mother that he had another double shift, so she didn't expect him at all."

"And the man was in your house?"

"Evil was in the house that night," he says. "All I remember was that Daddy came home, walked straight into their bedroom and snatched the covers off of both of them. He wanted to make sure it was true: That they were both butt-naked. He didn't want her to make any excuse about some kind of 'misunderstanding' or something."

"Oh no," I say. "You saw it all?"

"I saw Daddy snatch her up by the arm – and the dude grabbed his clothes and took off running like a punk. But Daddy took my mother and pushed her out the back door, with no clothes on."

"He pushed her outside naked?"

"Yep. Showed her right for messing around. They ended up in the garage arguing, so I couldn't hear all of it, but next thing I knew, they were divorced, the marriage was over – and we were living in South Central without Daddy."

I peek out the small cracks I make between my eyelids to steal a blurry glance at Geno, but his eyes are still closed, his expression reticent, waiting for my response.

"Something doesn't add up," I say. "How could you be so cold to your mother? Why are you so much on your father's side?

"Hey! What happened to no judgment?" he asks, incredulously.

"I'm sorry; forgive me?" I say, as if asking for a mulligan in a game of golf.

"Go on..."

"The thing is, I'm trying to get to the bottom of what really happened – like when you said your dad wanted to make sure it was true that your mom was cheating..." I trail off, putting the pieces together like Perry Mason.

"So?"

"And then you always call him 'Daddy' but never call her 'Mommy' or something endearing."

"That's just the way it was," he says, defensiveness growing in his voice.

"And why did your dad so happen to come home early when he said he had a double shift?"

"Men's intuition, I guess."

"Geno?"

"What?"

"Did you tell your dad that your mom was having an affair?" I ask.

Dead silence.

I open my eyes. He opens his. Jackpot.

"Geno, it's okay," I say, watching his mouth do a downturn, his face beginning to crumple into a mass of emotion. "You were a little boy. You did the right thing. You didn't know it would turn out like that."

He brings his head down as far near his lap as the phone will allow him. The undisputed sound of weeping traverses loud and clear across the phone line.

"I didn't know they would get divorced. I thought it would make everything better – like when you're in school and the teacher asks you if the person next to you copied off your paper during a test."

"I can't believe you've been carrying this burden by yourself for so long," I say.

"I did it for him. Daddy asked me what was going on at home, and I told him everything I knew. I went out on a limb for him," he sobs. "Then after I stuck my neck out, Daddy left us like we were yesterday's garbage. Moved on with his new life and new wife like it was so easy to forget us."

"You didn't see him again?"

"Only when he was dying of cancer, after it was too late for him to even speak. He'd already moved on and had his new family and forgot all about us – barely wanting to pay his child support. But he didn't realize, by punishing my mother – Mommy – he was punishing me, too."

"I'm glad he at least tried to apologize," I say.

"I wasn't trying to hear it. He'd left me with her – with that woman who called herself a mother. And she never let me forget I was the one responsible for our screwed up life."

"That wasn't fair of her, Geno. It was your mother's choice to have an adulterous affair, not yours."

"Tell that to her. She needed any excuse to punish me, blaming me for how her life turned out. My mother used to beat me for no reason – even waking me up out of my sleep by beating me."

"That's horrible."

"Who you telling?" he asks, looking directly into my opened eyes with anger. "What was even worse was the way she denied me. After the divorce, she was all scared that any new man would think she was too old, so she'd make me hide back in my room and not come out so the guys wouldn't know she had a son my age."

I purse my lips, taking in the insightfulness of what this grown man is telling me, the pains of a young boy finally brought to the forefront. "I want to rectify what you've gone through. I know only God and Jesus can take away your pain. On behalf of all women, may I say: *I'm sorry*."

The dam of tears breaks, and the levy that held back long buried emotions allows them to pour forth.

"I'm done," he says. "I'm so done."

"I know it seems that way, Geno, but in reality, this is just the beginning. Hurting people hurt people. Now that you've uncovered the source of your pain, and the reasons why you used it to hurt others, you can move forward and use it to help others – and yourself."

"How?" he looks up and asks, in a way that's so gentle, it's as if that 9-year-old boy has at last received some kind of recompense and hope for the pain and confusion he's experienced.

"You'll see soon. Great job."

Chapter 6:

Cash Rules Everything Around Me

Geno is staring at me, head on, wide-eyed, all ears. If it were legal for me to grab his face for emphasis and place both his cheeks in my palms, I would do so. For now, a left hand on the shoulder is as far as I will push it in this special interview room we've once again been granted inside the prison.

"I must know – forget all the religion, the church stuff, the religious rules and everything," I say. "I need to know that you've accepted Christ as your Savior, Geno."

"Yeah," he says, shrugging, looking away.

"No, no, no," I say, the seriousness of my tone forcing his eyes back toward mine. "I mean for real, Geno. If – heaven forbid – you had to die today, are you sure you're going to heaven?"

"Yes," he answers resolutely, a little bothered.

I wonder what that attitude is all about, but I breathe a sigh of relief all the same.

"What's the big rush?" he queries, furrowing his brows at me, with his wrists chained together. "Do you know something I don't know?"

"No, I haven't gotten any execution orders information," I say quietly. "You know I'll tell you the second I hear anything."

He slumps in relief as well. "I know."

"I've just had the feeling I needed to get that out of the way. Now we can move forward."

"Move forward to what?"

I hem and haw, looking down at my feet before glancing back up into his willing and eager-to-listen face.

"Well, you know, ever since you told me about your mom still being alive, I couldn't help but think about grief recovery."

"What's grief recovery?" Geno asks.

"You know STERBS and all that? Writing letters?"

"STERBS?" he asks. "What kind of language are you speaking, woman?"

"I forgot; you haven't really been hanging around the church crowd all up in here. STERBS is an acronym for 'short-term energy relieving behaviors,' which means the stuff we do that can be harmful in order to de-stress – like overeating, smoking, or indulging in angry outbursts."

"And why are you telling me all this?" he asks. "How does this relate to my case?"

"It will look good for you to have as many people on your side wanting to get your death sentence commuted as possible, especially a member of your family, like your mother. And in grief recovery, it shows us how to balance out all the good stuff a person did with the bad, so we can move past the hurt and forgive – and not have to rely on those 'STERBS' so much."

Geno is considering my words, but his face speaks of trouble from deep within, in that space beyond what he felt when speaking of his father. No doubt he would react this way, because it is said that issues with dads may float on the surface, but mother issues reside much deeper, in a place people don't often want to touch if there's bad feelings therein.

"All I can do is my part for reconciliation and forgiveness," Geno says. "Believe me, I've tried. But the rest is on her. You know what I'm saying?"

"She's never visited you all these years?"

Geno shakes his head, looking as if he could cry.

"Wow. One of the major tenets of Christianity has to do with forgiveness. How can you expect others to forgive you for killing Lasso and commute your death sentence when you're not willing to at least talk to your own mother?"

"I'm willing to talk to her now – I wasn't before," he says. "She was the one who wouldn't forgive me for 'abandoning' her when I went out on the road and made it big. After Daddy died, I was *done*. You feel me? I sent her gifts and things and she'd send them right back to me. That woman is a trip."

"Maybe she's changed..." I venture, trying to convince myself. "Maybe we could try and see...I mean, your dad changed over time."

"My dad only wanted me to forgive him on his deathbed. You see what I'm saying? That's when he finally 'got it' and realized he needed to make amends."

"Do you realize if this execution goes through, this is your deathbed right now?" I ask.

Something about the statement strikes Geno right in the heart. "Find her for me, and see if she's still alive. If you can get her to come out here, I'll talk to my mother. I can forgive her – for everything."

"Good deal," I say, invigorated with a new challenge to conquer.

§ § §

"Miss Thelma?"

Geno has already told me the proper greeting to use for his mother that she would no doubt find polite, so it's the first thing I say upon calling her, after spending plenty of time researching her whereabouts and at last digging up her landline phone number.

"Who is this?" she asks, the suspicion so evident in her tone.

"I'm a friend of your son Geno; my name is Alexa."

Dead silence.

"He wants to see you," I say, and wait. "Hello?"

I pull my smartphone away from my left ear and turn the face of the phone towards me. The time has stopped counting forward; the call has ended. I flip through the screen listing my recent calls and redial the same phone number I've just called.

"Miss Thelma?" I repeat, as soon as I get the inclination she might be on the other line, before she even says a word. "I think our call dropped."

"Nothing dropped, I just don't have anything to say to you," she snaps. "I know who you are. What's that y'all say to reporters? Oh yeah: *No comment.*"

"Wait, Miss Thelma, please," I beseech her with my own softened tone. "Geno really wants to see you. I know he misses you. He's willing to extend the olive branch."

She lets out a huff. "*Puh-lease!* I should be the one extending the olive branch to him – after all he's done. Now he wants to talk – after all this time. Why now?"

"I think there are a lot of things you two could say to one another, about the past and everything. You know, unresolved issues."

"Things are resolved in my mind," she quips, growing louder and more negative with every sentence. "Geno chose his father's side since he was a little boy – and as soon as he could get away from me, he did."

"He tried…" I offer. "He sent you gifts and everything once he was able."

"Is that what he told you?" she snaps. "Geno can't buy my love. Besides, you'd better watch out for him. He'll fool you like he's fooled a million other little girls over the years."

"It's not like that. That's not what I'm here for," I say. "You see, we've got this coalition started where we want to get him off death row."

"What? Are you kidding me? He's right where he deserves to be! He took a man's life."

"I know, Miss Thelma, but there was so much more to it than that," I say, frustrated, running out of words. "He could die. Your son could *die*. Don't you want to see him again? Talk to him at all?"

"I don't need to see Geno. I've said all I've needed to say to him," she says, coldly. "And he said all he needed to say to me the day he walked out of my life for that BWO crap."

"But people change. God forgives – why can't you?" I ask, knowingly overstepping my bounds.

"*God forgives – why can't you?*" she mocks, offering an overly exaggerated version of a whining voice.

Silence once more.

I look at my phone again, realizing that the call's time has stopped once more, but this time I understand most resolutely that it's not because the call has dropped.

No, Geno's mother has hung up on me once more – and this time, I do not call her back.

§§§

"No dice," I tell Geno the second I sit down in front of him. "I don't understand. How can a mother be so cold?"

"I told you," he says, putting on a brave face to hide the hurt. "That's my mother for you. Real talk."

"But you're her *son*," I say for emphasis. "Isn't the prospect of death supposed to make people treat you better? I mean, yes, people can get on each other's nerves and we take each other for granted and all that – but once we understand that we may not see a person again this side of heaven, usually that makes people soften a little."

"Not my mother. She's a perpetual victim; she's comfortable in that role," he notes. "Mix that philosophy in with a whole lot of anger and you've got this big mixture of a person who thinks everyone is out to get her or do her wrong, so she's not letting anybody else in – ever – unless Jesus Christ Himself comes down and tells her to."

I shake my head and study the table. "What a sad state of being. Perhaps she'll eventually come around as the time draws near."

Geno nods his chin up and down quickly, as if greeting an old friend. "*You* what they call an optimist, huh? I'm glad you've got enough positivity for both of us. When she said she wasn't letting nobody else in her heart, she meant that stuff – even her own flesh and blood."

I reach in my black Coach mailbag to remove a stack of paperwork and printed articles.

"That reminds me, I've been doing plenty of research into trying to get a stay of execution. We could have another chance at getting Prop 34 passed – perchance the death penalty could be repealed and replaced with life sentences without the possibility of parole. It almost passed in November of 2012 – who says it can't pass now?"

"I guess it could," Geno says. "I know all of us were really watching that vote closely."

"I didn't even pay much attention to it," I say. "I hadn't met you yet. But besides, even people who believe in the death penalty don't want to pay all this money for it. They may think in black or white – but they are voting based on green. Shoot, that's about $4 billion that taxpayers have been paying for all the stuff that comes along with the death penalty."

Geno looks skyward, as if trying to recall something. "Money is the answer to everything, right?"

"We've been all up in Ecclesiastes lately, haven't we?" I laugh.

"It's true," Geno answers. "It's like you don't always see all the wisdom in the Bible sometimes until you really need it."

I thrust a printed article with a blurry color photo of a Caucasian man near Geno's face.

"Look – this one guy got his execution delayed because he said he would donate his organ to his mother," I explain. "But that's just a rescheduling of a death date. We want yours done away with totally."

I shuffle through more papers to find another printed article, which I hold up at Geno's line of vision. He squints to read the headline as I hold my own wrist with my free hand to steady the paper for him to read, before finally placing it down on the table in front of him.

"Here's another serial killer who got a stay of execution from a judge," I say. "This one argued that the lethal injection would be too painful, cause too much suffering, and take two hours to kill a person."

"Are you serious?" he asks, his eyes growing wide with fear. "Is that for real?"

"I didn't even want to tell you this stuff – but I remembered I promised you that I wouldn't hold anything back. Besides, if this battle is successful, you'll hear it in the news anyway, so I wanted to tell you our game plan first."

Geno nods, giving me silent permission to continue passing along my research findings to him.

"According to the latest news reports, California still hasn't cleared the single-drug execution method – so that means they might still use the three-drug method. Look at these drugs: sodium pentothal, pancuronium bromide, potassium chloride..." I shake my head, trying to pronounce all the foreign sounding words. "People claim these are torture."

Geno clucks.

"How could serial killers and cold-blooded murderers still be sitting in prison after all these years – but I'm staring down my date of execution and all this lethal injection mess now?" he asks me. "What kind of sense does that make?"

"This has obviously grown to something larger than you, Geno," I tell him. "When something makes no kind of sense – it must have a deeper message involved. Your case could potentially overturn capital punishment laws in the state of California – heck, the whole United States – so folks are gathered on either side of the issue. There have already been so many states that have overturned their death row penalties, but people are looking at California as some sort of standard, as if wherever Cali goes, so goes the whole nation."

"They haven't killed anybody here on death row since 2006 – and they plan to make me the first one since then?" Geno asks rhetorically. "I ain't feeling it, I tell you."

"Crazy," I say.

"What about you?" he pauses, seemingly for great effect. "What side are you on? Do you believe in the death penalty?"

"I'll tell you the truth, in some cases I do," I say, not willing to lie to appease his feelings and fears. "Remember how Ecclesiastes says 'a time to die'? – I do believe there are some people who are so evil, so unwilling to change, so completely given over to the devil that to kill them would be a blessing to this Earth."

Geno twists his mouth sideways and sucks his teeth against the inside of his cheek. "Cold blooded. Ice cold. Sounds like some dudes I seen growing up in my neighborhood."

"But I do not believe you are one of those people."

He relaxes, as if a judge has seconds ago overturned his death row stay and rescued him from the death chamber.

"We did hit that book of the Bible hard, didn't we?" Geno asks, making a joke out of the serious situation – in that same way that he does when the room and topic gets too heavy.

"Yes we did, now let's lean on those promises to make more progress."

"Hey, I'm following you, Miss Lady A."

"Follow me as I follow Christ, a'ight?"

Geno nods, unable to josh any further.

§ § §

"If Geno has to be the poster child for death penalty opponents to get behind, so be it," I say to an *Associated Press* reporter who has gathered at the anti-death penalty rally location on the north side of the California State Capitol steps in Sacramento.

Pastor Prince, Swag-a-tarrius and a large group of others have become a peacefully boisterous group that has drawn the attention of the media and passersby in cars, on bikes and walking on foot.

Signs that say things like "Stop this legal lynching" and "Free Geno Cide" join others that read "Forgive Geno!" and the words "Death Penalty" crossed out in red.

Horns honk in support of our crowd as reporters with a crew carrying broadcast cameras hoisted over their shoulders approach us.

"Oh boy," I say under my breath, but not quiet enough under the din of the noise made by the rallying crowd that Pastor Prince doesn't hear my trepidation.

"Just open your mouth and God will fill it," he advises. "He always prepares a ram in the bush."

"I know," I say, "I just wish we had an even larger crowd – you know, some kind of momentum that would really put this thing over the top."

"I think you found her," Pastor Prince says, nodding toward a small female figure that catches the attention of the reporters, who shift their focus toward her.

It's Kim Stone, Dee's mother.

"Ms. Stone! Ms. Stone!" one reporter calls out, giving his cameraman the cue to start filming. "Are we rolling?" he asks the man.

"Yes," Kim says at the same time the cameraman nods in the affirmative.

"Now – we first and foremost want to offer our condolences for the loss of your daughter, Dee Stone."

"Thank you," she says, sadly smiling at the mention of Dee's name.

"Can you tell us why you came out here to join this rally and support Geno Stone, your former boyfriend?" he asks.

"Well, Geno is so much more than an ex-boyfriend to me," Kim says. "He's the father of my child, and we've been through so much together in life. Even though we couldn't make it as a couple, and even though we made mistakes as parents – I still believe there is hope left, and I don't want to give up on Geno. I don't think he deserves to die. Not like this."

"Well, apparently plenty of people feel the same way you do, as witnessed by rallies like these taking place all over the country. Why do you think that is? Why this case? Why this point in time?"

Kim looks around, as if she's taking in the enormity of the situation for the first time. "I believe people have put themselves in Geno's shoes. Of course he's a famous rapper – or at least, he was – and people have their own feelings about that. But as a parent, people have probably thought about the things they'd do if someone hurt their daughter…" she trails off into tears.

The male reporter reaches out his free hand to comfort her. "It's okay, we can only imagine how difficult this must be for you."

Kim composes herself and continues. "Thank you. It's really hard. But I believe somehow Dee would want me to be here, supporting her father."

§§§

Inside "Save Geno Central," as we've dubbed the conference room at the church that's the hub of the administrative arm of the fight to get Geno off death row, a group of us gathers around to watch the same interview with Kim that has been uploaded to YouTube and is gaining steam.

"Look at that," Swag-a-tarrius says, pointing to the view count beneath the video. "That one already has 250,000 views – and it was just uploaded yesterday!"

"People are really on this," I say. "I'm tripping that she even showed up."

"Expect God to do great miracles," Pastor Prince says.

The crowd disperses, each person off to his or her own task of answering phones, preparing more T-shirts, bumper stickers, or performing online work.

I sit motionless, staring ahead through the computer screen, long after Kim's interview has ended.

"What has your wheels turning now?" he asks. "I can tell something is up."

"Think about it, Pastor. If Dee's mother would join, what about the crazy notion of Lasso's mother actually joining the fight to save Geno's life?" I ask.

Pastor Prince jerks backward, as if the words have literally blown him back like a big force of wind. He puts a hand to his growing goatee and moves his fingers up and down along the hairs.

"Wow, now that would be something. Have you talked to Lasso's mom?" he says pensively.

"Not yet," I say, "but you told me to expect miracles."

"You'd have to tread carefully – I mean, asking the mother of the man who was murdered to support getting the man who murdered him off death row is a big pill to swallow," he says.

"I know, but maybe we can tag team her – visit her together like we did Geno. If God wants it and the power of the Lord is there, so be it," I say.

"Let's do it."

§§§

Betty Bridgeport is youthful looking, but a prim and proper type of woman – not the kind that you'd expect to have had endured the heartbreak of losing a son so young.

"Here's Lucas when he was three," she says, holding open a worn photo album to reveal a picture of a smiling boy riding around on a yellow and red Big Wheel. "He loved that thing."

"Cute," I say, taking a sip of the green tea she has offered, placing the porcelain cup back gently down upon the glass coffee table in her living room.

"You could tell he was a star even then, huh?" Pastor Prince asks, shifting his body next to us on the same couch, making noisy squeaks as the plastic covering the couch shifts along with his weight.

"I could," Betty says, grinning and touching the photo of the little boy as if caressing the face of her child in person. "A mother sometimes knows. Plus, God showed me in a dream that Lucas would rap before millions."

"And that he did," I say, keeping up with the conversation and all the while taking in our surroundings.

Everything about the young mother is an anomaly. Being the 40-something-year-old mom of a deceased rap star who'd made it pretty big and far in the game before having his life cut short, Betty would seemingly reside in a place that rivaled the modern mini-mansions of reality TV stars.

Instead, here we sit, inside the everyday kind of non-descript smaller home you'd find in a bunch of California neighborhoods. No winding driveways or expansive compounds. No, Betty's home is quite compact, with a neat yard and plush inside, decorated like someone's grandmother's overheated apartment. Comfortable, cute and unassuming, like the woman herself.

"It was only me and Lucas living here," she says, as if explaining the surroundings that she sees me taking in. "When he made it big, he wanted to buy me a new house, but I told him no. I tried to get him to save his money – everything's not what you'd expect in the rap game."

"How do you mean?" Pastor Prince probes.

"You know: the big houses, the fancy cars, the girls – all that stuff you see in the videos. Most of the time those are things that have been rented only for the video shoot for that day. They don't own none of that stuff," she laughs. "They're just flossing, as Lasso used to say."

We remain quiet, giving the grieving mother time to talk and reminisce.

"So I told my son not to fall victim to all that fakery. I didn't want him to think about trying to keep up with the next guy and have to outdo the image of what he thought he should be," she says.

"Did he listen to you?" Pastor Prince asks, like a solemn and quiet counselor.

"Not always," she says. "Not hardly. Lucas had a mind of his own. He thought I was behind the times. But just because I didn't know all the texting language and new lingo – like getting 'snatched' or being 'on my grind,' didn't mean I still didn't know right from wrong."

"It's not your fault, you know," I say out of nowhere. "I thought you should know that."

"I do," Betty says, looking me straight in the eye, surprised. "I know it and I tell myself that. But thank you for saying it out loud. It helps when people tell me that."

She reaches for a Kleenex from the box that sits on her coffee table and uses it to dab the inside corners of her eyes before continuing.

"I'm not one of those moms who's going to blame everything that happened to Lucas on other people," she says. "Yes, he got in with a bad crowd – but I don't blame them. I don't blame his father, and I don't blame myself. I don't even blame Geno."

Both Pastor Prince and I are taken aback by her words, and without looking at each other we can sense something happening in the atmosphere.

"Can we pray?" he asks, jumping on the opportunity.

"Sure," Betty says, and the three of us naturally reach out to hold hands, close our eyes and bow our heads in sync.

"Father God, we come before you to lift up Sister Betty in her time of love and remembrance of Lasso," he begins. "We are asking that you guide us all in what to do, where to go next, and show us how to not allow Dee's death and Lucas' death to have happened in vain. Let us not now lose Geno, too, without your hand of grace being over the situation. Continue to guide us and help us, in Christ's name we pray."

"Amen," our trio says in unison and we give each of the hands we're holding a squeeze, drop our grips, open our eyes and raise our heads.

"Lasso lived by the sword so he died by the sword," Betty says. "I told him he shouldn't love violence so much in his music – even in his relationships. So no, I don't blame anyone for his death. He made his own poor choices."

As she absentmindedly sweeps her hair back off of her temples, I study them, as if I'll see the telltale bruises that battered women wear. At this moment I begin to wonder if Lasso wasn't strictly violent with Dee alone – but if his own mother Betty is hiding secrets about how her son's volatile temper has hurt her in the past.

I wonder if that's why she's not mad at Geno...

"Thank you so much for your time," I say, rising to leave, surprising Pastor Prince, who rises also. "It's an honor to have met you."

I offer a weak and warm smile to Betty, reaching out to hug her. She embraces me fully, not letting go quickly, like someone who's bothered by human affection would do. Her hug is strong and genuine, a soul-to-soul kind of connection.

I know we came here to talk her into joining the fight for Geno's life, to turn her into some sort of interesting hook in a news story's plot line – parading Lasso's mother out for the world to see that she has forgiven Geno, too. But now that I've met her in person, and have witnessed her sweet and giving spirit firsthand, it's like I can't do it.

It feels too sleazy, like ambulance chasing or something seedy that I don't want to be a part of.

"Please keep in touch," I say, making my way to the door.

"But wait," she says. "You've got to give me the information about where to meet you guys."

"For what?" Pastor Prince asks.

"I want to join your team. I want Geno off of death row, too," she says. "I told you – I do not hold any hate in my heart towards him."

"We can do that, Betty," I say. "We can definitely do that."

"God is real!" exclaims Pastor Prince.

§ § §

"They are turning up the heat against you, Geno," I tell him at our next visit, after breaking the news about Betty joining the team – something he finds incredulous.

"How so?" he asks, eating with gusto, as he's been allowed to do in front of me this time, as if we are two coworkers having a corporate working lunch.

"The news is digging deep into your old lyrics to wage a mighty war against you – but it's really the death penalty fight at the heart of it all. They pulled some lines from your 'Don't F with My MRS' song."

"Oh boy," he says. "Which ones?"

I begin reading from a *Wall Street Journal* article. "Some niggas spend time discussing politics and religion. While I'm thinking about the next hot bitch I'm sticking."

"They printed that?"

"Hey, you wrote it!" I chastise.

Geno stops eating. "Man, it seems like a lifetime ago."

"I hear you. It's like we are literally different people from the ones we were all those years ago," I say.

"I wish the nation could see that," Geno says. "All some of them see is this scary rapper who they want to say 'Good riddance' to, as if that will cure all the ills of the world."

"Yeah, as if they're excising a bit of evil from the planet. But nothing's ever that simple. Well, at least Lasso's mom has ended up joining the fight for your life. And if your death sentence is found to not have been legally sound, we can hopefully get that stay of execution after all."

Geno pauses.

"Hey, tell me what you think about this," he perks up. "What if I reach out to some of the big name rappers I used to hang out with – you know, like Chill EP and Freeze Z and 'em?"

"Aw man that'd be awesome. I mean, they've transitioned from the rap world and are such big names in the acting world that having them as part of this movement would really bring it more attention," I say, getting excited.

"I haven't seen 'em in years, though," Geno remembers. "I hope I could get them to take my calls. Or at least get their agents to take my calls."

"Well, there's only one way to find out," I say. "It can't hurt to contact them to bring them on this 'Save Geno' campaign."

"Hell, they owe it to the world. We all made our money spitting those rhymes against women – and we've all made it seem like we had no part in the domestic violence and verbal abuse that followed some of our biggest fans who internalized that stuff."

"At least you recognize it and are repentant," I say.

"Yeah, that's what I want to tell Chill EP and Freeze Z, too. I mean, just because you transition on to a big movie career doesn't mean you don't owe some kind of apology for the crazy stuff we used to spit about females back in the day."

"That'd be great if they would show some remorse. You know, like the 'Million Man March,' where black men said, 'Look, we know we haven't always done right, but we're admitting it, apologizing and moving forward to do better in our communities.'"

"Right – just something, some kind of recognition."

"So let's do it," I say. "Having those major rap-turned-movie stars come out and offer apologies and then show they support you getting off of death row would make them a whole lot more palatable to society even more than they already are. And it might help your case tremendously."

"Do you think it could ever happen? Do you think there's any chance I could actually get off death row?" he asks. "Do you believe I might be able to get out of here someday?"

"I don't know, but I know we'd better keep pushing and trying. If we quit now, we have our answer already," I say. "But if we keep trying, anything could happen. We need some serious miracles."

"This kind come out only by prayer and fasting," he murmurs under his breath. Suddenly, Geno looks down at his food and pushes it away from him.

§§§

Geno's hunger strike has been effective. It has drawn the camaraderie of other prisoners across the nation, not only supporting his cause but to protest their own substandard conditions of living. He's even gotten responses from both Chill EP and Freeze Z, the former having agreed to pay off the satellite church building that serves as headquarters to the "Save Geno" struggle and donate money to the cause. The latter has also given $100,000 to the campaign – an amount that even Jeffrey (Geno's former manager DV-U$) also donated to the cause.

However, it's been 14 days, and I am worried about Geno's survival.

"People have died doing this," I say to him over the phone.

"The water tastes sweet," he says, slowly and weakly. "It's weird. I have to drink it really slowly. I've got sores in my mouth."

"I want you to eat something now," I beg. "You've brought even more attention to your case than ever before. It's an answered prayer that all these famous rappers have gotten up here to support your cause and apologize for their past rap songs. But you won't be able to help if you don't make it through."

"Okay, that's the sign I asked for," he says. "I prayed that you would tell me to eat, to know it's over. And here you are, telling me to eat."

"Get your strength back up. We'll visit soon."

§§§

"My execution date has been postponed!" Geno blurts out upon seeing me.

"I heard," I say, taking in how much better he looks and sounds than the last images I saw of him on the news, his face appearing gaunt and scrawny during his fast. "Boy, you look a lot better today."

"I feel so much better. It's like I've come off of the biggest spiritual fast I've ever taken, and so many things have shifted in my thinking over the past few weeks," he says.

"Oh yeah? Like what?" I ask. "The most I've ever really fasted was about five days, and even then it was so good. I love fasting, but I hate it, too."

"I hear you. Mine was rough, but necessary. It's like my focus is now clear," he says. "So if I don't make it – even though my execution is set for later – I want you to do something for me."

"Of course, I mean, don't think like that – envision a positive outcome of getting off death row," I say.

"Believe me, I am. But another part of me wants to prepare for the worst," he says, looking skyward. "Or the best, if it's meant to go that way."

"What do you want me to do for you, Geno?"

"First off, if I haven't said thank you for all you've done already, let me say it now: *Thank you.*"

"Of course," I say. "This is one book that has changed my life."

"Mine, too," he says. "And I don't mean that in a funny way. Looking back on my life like this has really helped me. But this is what I want you to do: I figured out that I might not have been able to save Dee from Lasso, but I can do my part in saving a whole bunch of other Dees from a lot more Lassos."

I give him a quizzical look. "What do you mean?"

"I want to start a foundation called 'Our Kids Keepers' and have it help young girls with their low self esteem, to let them know they are loved and cherished – and that they don't need a man to use them in order to feel validated."

"Wow, Geno, that's excellent – you really did do some soul-searching and praying during that hunger strike."

"I did. I kept begging God to show me how I can make it up to society, you know, all the damage I did with all my bad lyrics, my horrible lifestyle, and all the wrong ways I taught young men to treat young women."

"That's deep, and unique. You don't find a whole lot of rappers like you who spewed those misogynistic lyrics back in the day – or are still doing it – who later come back and apologize, or even admit what they did was harmful."

"Yeah, they think it's easier to just gloss over it and keep it moving like nothing happened and become the next mainstream movie star acting in a bunch of kids' movies like the perfect dads. But I realized that's why I was stuck and that's the type of thinking that landed me here in the first place. I had to take accountability and responsibility for my part in all this."

"Well call it done, my friend. 'Our Kids Keepers' it is," I say. "And I have met so many women and men as great resources who would be willing to really offer valuable insight to these young girls to help steer them in the right direction in life."

"That's all I want," he says, smiling, trying to wink away a small droplet of a tear before it falls. "I will give you and Kim the instructions to the trust I'd set up for Dee, where we can donate all the money to the mission in her memory."

"Dee would be proud."

"Now, back to the book," he says. "Did you find a good agent?"

"We've got lit agents beating down the door. But do you know what I think we should do, Geno?"

"What?"

"Publish it on Amazon ourselves, and keep this momentum going. Why turn all that power over to some publishing house that will sit on it for a year or two and then possibly change your whole story around?"

"I don't know," he says. "Why would we do that?"

"No good reason to do so. Since we've got all the chapters and you've read it all, we're ready to go. People could be buying it and reading it on their Kindle devices in about 12 hours after you give me the go ahead to publish the book. Even if you sell the print rights, you should keep your electronic rights, meaning the digital version of the book."

Geno looks amazed. "Man, things really have changed since I've been locked up in this joint. Life seems to move so fast out there and so slowly in here. Go ahead, put it up."

"You ain't said nothing but a word," I say. "I'll do it as soon as I get home."

§ § §

Geno's face takes up the entire cover of the book as I tweak and design it to perfection. He looks serious and a bit mean, but the photo shows a piercing soulfulness deep within his gaze.

It is the kind of book cover you cannot ignore, one that grabs a reader's attention as he or she absentmindedly scrolls through a long section of thumbnail-sized book covers for something interesting to read.

I upload a file to the Amazon Kindle Direct Publishing module called "Dying to Live Again," and begin previewing the book for correctness. The author name "Geno Stone" is displayed prominently on the front cover beneath his face, and within the title page as I flip and flip through each page, virtually, along with quotes from Geno intertwined with his old rap lyrics highlighting each page.

After entering the book's description field and various other information about pricing and rights, I click the button that reads "Save and Publish."

On the screen, a big and bold box appears with the wording "Publishing…" and warns, "Please be aware that it can take up to 12 hours for English and 48 hours for other languages to be available for purchase in the Amazon Kindle Store."

§ § §

"Hello, published author," I greet Geno, my Kindle in hand, the cover of his book displayed on the screen.

"That's actually it?" he says, beaming through the glass.

"That's it," I say. "It can be published that fast. And people are already buying it and leaving great reviews."

"I want to read it again, even though I've already read it," he says.

"I know…I do that, too. Especially with stuff I like that I've written. There's something about seeing it in this format instead of merely in the Microsoft Word document that makes it all the more real."

Geno continues to smile, beaming at his own "mean mugging" on the cover of his memoir, taking only a split second away to look at me and realize there is another big important bit of news I need to share.

"What is it?" he asks, curious.

"Now, I don't want you to get overly excited. This is only the beginning…"

"Just tell me! What?"

"You can reread your biography later. Right now we need to go over every detail about your case with a fine toothcomb. I mean everything – from when you were booked, tried and eventually sentenced to death for the first-degree murder of Lasso."

"Alexa – will you tell me what's going on?" Geno pressures me, getting more excited than frustrated. "You said you'd tell me all things, no matter what. I can handle it, good or bad. Or devastating?" he pries, trying to read my poker face expression.

"Because of all of the attention on your case, the book, the rallies, the protests, the rappers, the movie stars – and first and foremost, the grace of God alone – you've got a new fair sentencing hearing."

"Are you kidding me? You're not joking?"

"No; it's real. They want to make sure to pick out every detail of your case – because the public thinks that race played a big part in you receiving such a harsh sentence. Maybe we can see if there is anything there that can get your death penalty reversed."

"Aw, man, I pray it's true. I pray," Geno says, shaking his head like he doesn't even want to hope to believe, as if opening the door to the possibility of him getting off of death row will somehow jinx his chances and work in reverse.

"Why not you, Geno? Don't we all deserve a second chance in life? Everybody has made mistakes."

"Yeah, but maybe not as big as mine."

"Well, that'll be up to the judge to decide," I tell Geno, clarifying, "and I ain't talking about a human judge."

He takes in a large, long deep breath and holds it for several seconds before letting it out slowly.

"All right, let's go forward, with love."

Chapter 7:

When You Hit the Bricks...

"If you got out of here today, what would be the first thing you'd do?" Pastor Prince asks Geno, and it reminds me of one of the first questions I planned to ask him the first day I visited death row.

Geno, however, remains quiet – as if he were an injured inmate refusing to rat out the folks on the yard who hurt him. I don't understand this silence; this quietness is not blessed. I haven't mentioned our phone conversations, and I'm hoping that by glossing over them Geno will pick right up where we left off during our last visit, not from our harried and hurried phone conversations. However, he's not having any of it, even ignoring his best friend.

"I told you not to come here the last time we talked," he says to me. "You know I said you can tell me everything over the phone from now on until I tell you otherwise."

"But why? You know I hate those phone calls and getting interrupted by recordings and everything," I say. "I don't get it. Why have you been avoiding me? Why have you been denying my visits? I though you liked having me visit you."

"Real talk time, man," Pastor Prince interjects. "What'd we do?"

Geno looks beyond us, out through a decrepit window with bars that afford an abbreviated view out onto the lower yard, where men mill about in groups, seemingly segregated by their races – some yards populated with men in orange shirts, others with men in blue gear painting the backdrop of the concrete.

He looks back nervously at both of us. "The book is over and published. We don't have to meet so much in person anymore. Our talks don't require that much time together now."

"Did I tell you it hit #1 on Amazon?" I ask, trying to divert away from his weird mood. "And it made a lot of other best-selling book lists."

"God's favor is on this book," Pastor Prince says, pointing a long index finger down at the table as if the book were right there in front of him. "Seriously; I mean it."

Geno nods, but his gaze remains trained on the window as he paces in small back and forth lines in the spacious yet rickety room we've been given to continue our meetings within during this visit – and this visit alone. It seems each visit brings a fresh locale in the run down place, and none of the visits are short of some sort of drama, either real or perceived in varying levels of intensity.

A guard stands armed near the wall with an actual gun and a pepper spray gun that looks like a high-powered onyx rifle. His radio walkie-talkie crackles with scratchy voices transmitting various codes back and forth. The guard glances constantly from Geno out to the yard and back again.

"I know that we don't need to meet about the book anymore, but we still have a long journey to go with your possible exoneration or death sentence being commuted," I say.

Pastor Prince chimes in. "I'm still hoping for the best. I want you to get released. You know, to think hopefully about living again on the outside. See Fisherman's Wharf and Pier 29 once more. You're not giving up are you?"

Geno looks at both of us and then lets out a sigh. "It's not that. You know that saying that snitches get stitches? That's what's been on my mind. Not any fanciful thoughts about playing around in North Beach somewhere."

"Has somebody been threatening you?" the man of God asks, hulking up as if to report his child was being bullied to the school principal.

"What do you mean, Geno? Who's the snitch in this scenario? Me or you?" I ask.

"Well, it would be me, if I told you that I noticed the odd behavior going on in the prison lately," he confides, lowering his voice, looking around him although we are the only three people in the room with the armed officer.

"Like what?" I ask, suddenly intrigued with the shift in his secretive and solemn demeanor.

"People have been stocking up on food in here," he says resolutely, as if he's given me the answer to the meaning of life.

"Oh," Pastor Prince pulls his head up and down slowly.

"So what are you trying to say? What does that mean?" I ask, hoping he will speak plainly.

"You can't ever get used to this place, y'all. This isn't a camp or a dorm or a hotel or someplace fun. This can be hell on earth, or at least feel like a nice version of Hades at times. And that's not saying anything good about this place; it's only speaking to how horrible hell really must be compared to this above-ground hellhole."

"You got it brother," Pastor Prince reaches out to place a hand on a crumbling portion of the concrete wall, then looks up to the pipes wrapped with deteriorating protective covers hanging over our heads, threatening to drop asbestos on us at any moment.

"Believe me, after I watched the documentaries about San Quentin, I barely wanted to come in here," I say. "But I came anyway – for your story. So Geno, just say what you want to say. Talk to me like I'm a two-year-old."

"All right look – if the yard starts to get quiet like it's been getting quiet and you see guys stocking up on food, you know it's not a good sign. When there's tension in the air, you can feel it..." Geno says.

We follow his stare out that same window, trying to discern if the normally noisy and boisterous place sounds any more peaceful to my ears. It still sounds like a cacophony of noises to me – a symphony of too many men in too small of a confined space with too many emotions and spirits boiling over.

"When everything's fine, usually everybody's talking and laughing. But you can definitely feel it when trouble is brewing. Unfortunately, that's something I've come to learn well in my many years inside the walls of this penitentiary. Even from here, I can see the way certain ones gather in groups and start whispering. Even from far away, I can feel that vibe."

"We get those prophetic warnings for a reason," Pastor Prince says, straightening up and studying the figures in the yard.

I begin to understand the enormity of what he is telling me, and all at once the rush of fear mixed with excitement begins to bring flashes of the scenes I've seen in many YouTube videos about life in San Quentin to my mind.

Before I can verbalize my thoughts, a shrill alarm sounds. Geno automatically sits on the ground, but I freeze in a standing position, looking at the guard for direction. A post-fear rush of adrenaline makes my tongue numb, like the time in college when I nearly got into a collision with another car. But this accident isn't nearly avoided – here lies before us the curious anticipation of a plight that only one of us expected.

Pastor Prince makes a beeline for the door, but pauses before opening it and turns back around for guidance.

"Stay down," the guard firmly says to Geno, as the man points his weapon in Geno's direction, while at the same time he listens to the urgent calls on his radio. "Come with me," the guard tells Pastor Prince and me, but doesn't move right away. Instead, he keeps his ear on high alert, listening like a protective dog at the ready for his master's call.

"Code 3! Code 3!" The voice over the static-sounding air is insistent. "All personnel report now. We need all personnel. Lockdown situation."

The guard glances down at Geno, who is still crouched on the floor and back at us visitors, and makes a split decision as he yells to all of us, "Stay here and don't move out of this room!"

§§§

Lockdown.

It's the familiar wording you hear but never think of experiencing.

"I've finally stopped shaking," I tell the men through the darkness of the room. Fading natural light seeping through unintended skylights made by cracks in the ceiling is some of our only light in the entire space. For the prison's lights have dimmed, as if they are those in a home hit by a storm that has knocked out the power – one that's being run by a generator.

"Good," Geno whispers, pausing as the noise of boisterous male voices approaches, and the sound then travels down the hallway beyond the closed door of the room.

"Remain as still as possible," Pastor Prince says under his breath in my direction.

"I will," I whisper back. "My ex-husband taught me that it is motion that draws the eyes of people. He was in the army. Special Forces. So let's be still."

"And know that he is God? Amen!" Geno says, trying to sound confident.

"Psalm 46:10," Pastor Prince confirms, trying to keep the mood light, but his voice betrays a bit of shaking, too.

§§§

The three of us are sitting up against the wall in a nook shaped like a small closet that has no door, so it is easier for us to hear the various voices and sounds of movement of people as they pass by every blue moon outside the door of this special room we used today.

As soon as we all heard "Code 3" however, the code for a serious prison riot situation, we knew this would be no ordinary day at San Quentin. My mind whirls with plenty of different scenarios of how this could play out, as a writer's brain often does.

"I wonder why the guard hasn't come back yet," I ask, though I already know the most likely reason.

"It'll be okay," Geno says, as we all twist our backsides on the floor to allay the numbness of sitting for hours.

"God wouldn't bring us this far to leave us now," Pastor Prince declares, sounding calmer after our long time of silence.

I exhale, trying to make out their eyes in the darkening light. "It's okay – I know you're both trying to put on a brave face for me. But if I have to tell you the truth, Geno, you need to tell me the truth, too."

"All right," Geno says, his tone growing more serious as he still keeps his voice to a very low volume. "They must not have the riot secure yet, or else they would've long come back and got me and brought me back to my cell and have taken y'all out of here. There must be more pressing issues more important than me right now. Besides, since I'm not a part of the general population anyway – and I'm like a super-protective custody case – it's best for all of us to stay way the hell out of sight."

I keep my voice down as well as I whisper near his face. "That's what I've figured."

"Has this happened before, man?" Pastor Prince asks.

"It's not my first riot here," he says wistfully, "but I hope it ends soon – these guys in here can be downright nasty. They gassed this one guard years ago and he quit that same day."

"How did they get ahold of gas?" I ask, imagining either a bucket full of gasoline or some kind of mist.

Despite himself and the dire situation, Geno lets out a slight and ironic chuckle. "I forgot you two don't know the ways of prison life. Gassing means they take feces and urine and let it rot for days and get so gross that you don't even want to think about it. They threw it at the man. And some of these dudes have Hepatitis C and HIV...that's why the officers have those newer face masks covering their whole heads, necks and everything."

I press my head back against the hard wall and think of home. A soft and firm king-sized bed, t-shirt jersey flannel sheets and a delightful bedroom of peace is the exact place I wish I could close my eyes and transport myself to right now – an oasis of safety and comfort. Oddly, I think of bringing Geno with me, too, not for any evildoings, but simply to continue this compelling conversation that I don't want to have in this specific location this exact evening. There is a wild atmosphere to this place tonight, and I think of Geno having to endure the uncertainty of riots like this before and feel a strong level of empathy for him, unlike days before.

"I can't believe you've had to live like this for so long man," Pastor Prince says. "I'm sorry I haven't visited you as much as I should have before."

"Nobody can do anything to me. They can only kill me once," Geno says, picking up on the fact that his long-time friend is trying to offer some kind of amends – just in case.

"I know we're not supposed to be afraid of people who can only kill our bodies and not our souls. This is scary, though," I say, jumping as I hear unidentified sounds.

Geno turns as if trying to make out my face in the darkness. "I think it's just so many people, all crowded into one place. So many spirits and souls and there's frustration. It seems to percolate and blow up eventually."

"I get that, like when so much stress builds up inside, and you're carrying around all this nervous energy. That's when I like to jump on the treadmill and knock out a 5K," I say.

Geno speaks through the dusky atmosphere. "Oh man how I miss the treadmill. It's those little things you don't even think about till you don't have access to them anymore."

"My thing is knocking the heck out of a golf ball," Pastor Prince says. "You got to do something to get the anger out."

"Why do some people want to lash out so much though?" I ask. "I heard about that one guy who slashed that officer's hand after the guy pretended to drop his mail in his cell and he reached for a shank instead."

"That's it, case in point," Geno says. "You can never drop your guard in here. You can never get used to it, like it's a home or something. You've got to form a thick skin in here."

"Yeah, and wear a lot of riot gear. I saw that other prisoner on TV that shot a dart out at that guard through his food portal."

"Some guys are crazy. That's all there is to it," Geno says. "But you know what? Part of it for me is like an extension of growing up in South Central. I've been watching my back all my life. It's nothing really new to me. It's true to me. At least the self protection part."

"Well this is all new to me. Stay close," I say.

"You were kind of soft when you came to the neighborhood," Pastor Prince jokes.

Geno, however, apparently doesn't find it funny, because he lurches past me and grabs Pastor Prince's shirt. "Where were you, man? We were supposed to be boys!"

I can feel Geno's warm breath in the space in front of me, and almost see Pastor Prince's surprised reaction as he stammers.

"What the hell, Geno?"

"You left me up in here to rot!"

"I tried with you, man," Pastor Prince spits back. "I was trying with you from way back in the day – you were always so hardheaded. You had to learn the hard way."

"Man, ain't nobody was trying to get saved back then. I didn't even know what that meant," Geno says, his whisper growing louder. "But after I did, I thought you'd be all up in here, keeping my head up, man – seeing as though *you* supposed to be a *pastor* and all."

"Shhh…" I warn.

"Don't ever question my gift, Geno. I said I was sorry. I'm here now, man. I'm here now."

"Please," I whine as if my dam of emotions could melt into large and loud sobs at any moment. "We have to stay quiet."

Geno releases his grip on Pastor Prince and both men fall back against the wall once more, as if they completed a set of bench presses.

"I'm sorry, dude," Geno says. "I'm not ready to die. I don't want to die."

His pleas echo into the night, as if prayers sent out through every hole and open space they can find to float up and away from this place.

§ § §

A loud and rowdy cadre of men breaks through the dreamlike reverie state and puts Pastor Paul, Geno and me on high alert, as witnessed by the way our bodies sit up and stiffen against the wall. I hold in my breathing until they pass and the sounds of their cursing voices lessen. None of us were sleep, but we've stared off into the pitch-dark expanse of the room soundlessly for so long that it was kind of like entering the dazed state of a person who gets hypnotized by the dotted white lines of the road when they've been driving for hours down a highway. They may not be asleep, but they aren't fully awake, aware and alert either.

"If we had to escape from here, where could we go?" Pastor Prince asks, entertaining a thought that I know could very well become reality if this riot gets anymore out of control.

"Not the dungeons, please. What about if we could make it to the correctional officers' homes?" I ask.

"No," Geno says immediately. "Those are too far away, and the officers in the gun towers would have permission to shoot anybody they think is escaping."

He remains wordless for a few seconds, and I can almost imagine Geno mapping out the prison layout in his mind.

"We could try to make it to the garden chapel," he says. "It's real close, and I always feel better when I go there."

"I bet," Pastor Prince agrees.

"You can shout and get your praise on and get that emotional release for a couple of hours a week," I say.

"Being around all those believers must really help your spirit in a place like this, surrounded by so much evil going on," Pastor Prince says.

"Yeah. How ironic is it that you tried to get me to visit your church for years while I was on the outside – but I never would go. I thought my rap career was so much more important than that stuff you were talking. I made fun of your first little old church. Shoot, the first time I started going to church was when I got locked up."

"At least you turned around for the better," he answers.

"It's funny how getting sent to prison makes some people more violent than they were on the streets. But not you," I say to Geno.

"We got all types up in here, from the level one low risk peeps to the level four high risk ones – and you never know how it's going to turn out. But I know one thing, coming here and finally being in one place for a long period of time, and seeing all these different types of people made me stop judging other people so harshly," Geno says, sounding reflective.

"So what would be the first thing you'd do if you ever got out?" Pastor Prince probes once more.

"Aw, shoot. I don't even like to dare myself to dream about those things. But I'll admit, when it gets real quiet in here, I'll break down crying in my cell – and I try to keep it on the low – but I think about if I could've made it up to Kim, all the wrong I've done, you know? If I would've figured out what was important in life earlier, maybe things could've been so much different for us."

"Like how?" I probe.

"You might as well tell her. We've got the time."

"Okay, but it might sound like the silliest thing you ever heard coming from a man on death row," he says. "I think about if I could've just married Kim, and if she would've forgiven me for all the messing around and the groupies and stuff, maybe we could've had more kids – a real family."

"That doesn't sound silly at all," I say.

"Naw, man, that's real talk," Pastor Prince says. "Nearly every man wants that: forgiveness and a good wife."

"Well, this part might," he cautions. "I think about being a regular dad, you know, doing boring things. Like I could've come off of tour and could have gone grocery shopping and driven up the highway to pull up in the driveway of one of those cute houses. I didn't need a mansion or nothing."

"That sounds fun. And very normal for a fabulous rapper's fantasy," I try to joke and sound light, but my voice still betrays my fear. "Why didn't you tell me all this before? We could've put this in the book. Oh well, we can always do follow up articles. Tell me what you'd like to eat in this family fantasia."

"I'd bring home some Fatburger or In-N-Out – because prison food is so nasty that I think about that good food on the outside a lot – and when I'd get home, Kim would be there washing the dishes, looking out the kitchen window at our kids playing in the backyard. That's the stuff I think about."

"It makes perfect sense," I confirm.

"Yeah," Pastor Prince says. "A lot of your fans might've thought the life that you had was everything, you know, all that clubbing, raising those glasses, making it rain at the strip clubs. But I'll always remember what this one woman who survived Nazi Germany's death camps said when she told an audience that after that kind of experience, you learn to appreciate another 'boring' night at home."

"I get it," he says. "I only wish I'd gotten back then, when it mattered most, so I wouldn't waste all these years of my life doing—"

A loud bang like an explosion goes off in the distance, shocking us into silence once more. The distinct smell of chemicals and smoke eventually filters through our space. Geno places his hands up to cover his mouth and motions for us to do the same.

"Do you have any weapons?" I ask.

"No – I got rid of all my contraband. I didn't want anything standing in the way of my new sentencing hearing."

"Shoot, that's right," I say.

"I applaud your honesty – but you're telling me you have no tomahawks? No razor weapons? Nothing?" Pastor Prince asks with an urgent tone to his line of questioning.

"Don't worry," Geno calms us, "if we do have to leave this room unescorted, I'll bet you we can find a zip gun or something. And since we're all tall, we can reach up in the eye beams to look for hidden weapons. I see them up there all the time – I don't ever point them out, though."

"Snitches get stitches," I repeat.

"Yep – or instead they get set up in the private custody place we call PC – or in the SNY, the sensitive needs yard. That's where the ones who dropped out from gangs go. Or the transvestites, child molesters, or guys who said certain things to get there, for their own protection."

"This prison mentality is something else," Pastor Prince observes.

"It's a whole 'nother world," Geno says. "And to think, I only started acting like a gangster when we were young bucks because I saw that girls liked gangsters, and I loved the girls. If I could go back, I wouldn't be here."

"What would you be?"

"I'd be one of those nerds."

"Remember Riley, man?" Pastor Prince asks. "We thought he was so square."

"I know, with those pop-bottle glasses?" Geno asks. "Yeah man, the girls we used to mack to in high school didn't like those boys who were squares and nerdy and geeky, but now those are the ones running these multi-million dollar companies and stuff. And hard, pretty boy OGs like me are up in here."

"Or running churches," Pastor Prince laughs at himself.

Our trio chuckles quietly, breaking the tension slightly by distracting ourselves with humor. The gaseous fumes seem to fade from the room.

"I wish I could've put all this stuff in the book," I say, " but I'll just plan to save it for book number two, after your sentence is commuted."

"Yeah, we can call that one 'How to Remain Sane in a Four-by-Nine Foot Prison Cell.'"

I snicker, but I can tell Geno is turning deadly serious once more.

"I can't even stretch my arms all the way out sideways in my cell. And I'm sitting up here watching all these 3rd termers getting paroled," he says, and I can see the shadow of his head bowed low and shaking. "I hate this old and decrepit place. It's not like they have any electrified lethal fences – plus, they've got less surveillance cameras than convenience stores."

"It's got to be so tempting to want to be out of here. Especially with beautiful San Francisco Bay right outside the walls teasing you and taunting you."

"It's not right, but I see why people try to escape from federal prisons," Pastor Prince says, as if he's imagining what life would be like on the inside.

"I can't stand it. They stripped searched me when I first got here, made me spread my cheeks and all that degrading junk. They cut my hair low – and now they'll strip search guys right outside, with no privacy."

As Geno talks, I look around at the shadowy alcoves that are worn down around us, with the holes in the ceiling still providing light streaming in by what looks like the amber glow of streetlamp type of powerful lights.

"They still have to unlock the doors of the cells one at a time it's so old. The gun rail is a mess," he says. "But mainly, I'm going it alone because I don't belong to a gang. I stay away from the exercise yard and the lower yard and all those yard politics because of who I am."

"That must make for a lonelier existence," I note.

"It's not good for man to be alone," Pastor Prince says. "But then again, none of us is ever really alone."

"I'd rather not be involved. I mean, the brothers are all over the place – all segmented, even though there's so many of us. Some other races stick together, no matter what gang they were affiliated with on the streets. That's smarter, in my opinion. The Asians control a certain area and they've got titles like 'Minister of Defense' – the guy that has a bunch of weapons ready at all times, hidden all over the place."

"You are not making me feel better," I quip.

"You've really got to watch your back out there, huh?" Pastor Prince asks him, as if the danger of the place is finally sinking in.

"You all said you wanted the truth. Anyway, this is called the third watch of the night," Geno says, trying to calm me.

"Just like in the Bible," I say.

"Yeah, it's a trip how they call it the same thing," Pastor Prince says.

Suddenly, another noise makes us shut up and listen hard once more. The handle of the door to the room begins to move slowly, creaking with a weird solace that automatically lets me know we're rescued.

"We are in here," Geno says.

"Peacefully surrendering," Pastor Prince says.

"With visitors!" I say, with my voice pitched high so they'll know I'm a female.

Flashlights blind our vision, but in between the rays of glare I can make out the distinctive gear of the prison officers.

§ § §

"Back on Death Row" reads the headline of the San Francisco Chronicle article that Swag navigates to on her iPad as a small group of us – including Pastor Prince and Betty – stands around her in a circle inside the inner sanctum of the church.

"The fair sentencing hearing of popular rapper Geno Stone has landed him back on death row," she reads, and our shoulders collectively droop, listening to how the controversy surrounding the prison riot helped to reinforce public opinion – that apparently leaked into the courtroom – of dangerous criminals needing to be kept right where they are: locked away with one another, far away from us on the outside and placed on death row if need be.

Swag continues to read the article about what sounds like a foreigner to me, written from the perspective of a man who couldn't possibly have known Geno, only one giving his expert view based upon public records and other cold, concrete data – not from a person who has looked in the rapper's eyes and sat on the firm floor with him as he bared his soul in the darkness.

"Geno has survived prison riots," I say when Swag finishes reading the article to the group. "There are dangerous men in there who've done ten times worse the kind of things he did and they aren't even on death row."

Pastor Prince, Lasso's mother, Swag and the others stare at me, their eyes widened. I wonder if I've gone too far, wearing my heart on my sleeve and displaying too much raw emotion. I don't care.

"We've got to do something. The execution date has been scheduled again and everything! We've got to get him a stay of execution somehow," I say.

More stillness surrounds the group before Pastor Prince speaks up. "Why don't we create another kind of viral video? Maybe a rap video this time?"

"Let's do it now!" I nearly scream.

"We can grab some of his old music, but I can rhyme different lyrics in between and update it, you know," says Swag-a-tarrius. "You know I can spit something serious."

"We know you're very talented," Betty tells Swag.

"I can help write the lyrics," I say, feeling the fire of the dynamic group coming together for a common cause. "We could intersperse his old stuff – the meaningful parts – with new lyrics that celebrate his new way of thinking. And have Chill EP and Freeze Z spit a verse or two."

"I'll tell Geno as soon as I can talk to him again," Pastor Prince chimes in. "He can contribute lyrics, too. Make him feel like a big part of it all. I don't know when the last time it was since he wrote a rap song. This can give him a chance to reverse some of those horrible lyrics from the past."

"Then we can edit the video to make it look really nice," Swag says. "We can make it look professional."

"All right, y'all," Pastor Prince says. "Let's prepare to buckle down, because I've got service in the morning."

"*In the morning, when I rise,*" the group begins singing after his statement, one by one, impromptu, until there's a bunch of hand clapping and simultaneous foot stomping.

What began as a sort of mocking church service has turned real.

§§§

"You're telling me 4.5 million people have already watched that?" Geno says, smiling, watching the finished YouTube video titled "Let Geno Cide Live" via Pastor Prince's smartphone that he holds shakily across the table in the same special room where Geno and I spent so many hours during the riot.

"Yeah, man," he answers.

"Dude, I couldn't get that many viewers on MTV that easily after I dropped some of my first videos. Heck, they wouldn't play us at all for a long time."

"Things are definitely different with music these days, too," I add, "especially the way they break new and independent artists."

"So this is Swag-a-tarrius, huh?" Geno asks, bobbing his head to her beats and rhymes as she makes a cameo appearance in the video during her specific parts.

"Yes, Geno, this girl is going all out for you," Pastor Prince says. "She's a big reason for this video going viral – and as a result of more notoriety to your case, for your stay of execution being ordered."

Geno drops his head briefly, forcing himself to look back up again, from me to Pastor Prince and back. I get the feeling it is time for me to step away, so I do, pretending that I'm not still in earshot within this room, which is spacious when compared to a prison cell – or "house" as it were – but not when it comes to the average size of one's living room or master bedroom in a home.

"What is it, man?" I can hear the pastor saying emphatically.

"I want to live, dog," Geno's voice quakes as he talks. "I want to live."

"It's looking hopeful. I can't promise you the moon but it is looking better than it's looked in years.

"When I get the chance, I want to thank Swag-a-tarrius," Geno says. "In fact, please thank her again for me?"

"I got your back, dog," Pastor Prince says, trying to keep upbeat.

"I never would've imagined – a lesbian rapper, fighting this hard for me? I used to call women like her such bad names. I didn't think nothin' 'bout 'em man. I probably dogged them worse as punishment for not swinging 100% my way."

"None of us knew how to be real gentleman back then."

Geno squeezes his eyelids tightly together, as if shutting off the spout to a faucet with extra strength. "It is amazing to me that I just played women like objects – I played with them like chess pieces – and I always thought I was the one getting over on them."

"You're finally starting to see them more as human beings?"

"Even more than I thought I ever could," Geno admits. "Not every lady is some piece I need to hit. I see that now. I used to throw them away like dolls a kid got tired of playing with – but look who's mostly riding hard for me through my whole ordeal and trying to get me up out of here."

"Women?"

"Women. And you man," Geno says.

"Road dog, boss hog," Pastor Prince smiles.

§ § §

As quickly as the stay of execution brought Geno's hopes up – along with all of the hopes of his supporters – it seemed nearly as fast that a federal court of appeals overturned and flat-out reversed that same order that canceled Geno's execution.

It took a panel of a few judges to summarily rule that the other United States judge that had stayed Geno's original execution had ruled without a basis for delaying his death.

"This is such an emotional up and down," I say to Pastor Prince, as a small group of us has gathered in the church's rectory to process this unexpected news. "I can't imagine how Geno is feeling. If he'd committed a crime against somebody who hadn't killed his daughter, I'd feel differently. I guess I wouldn't feel so sorry for him."

"Me too," Swag says. "This case feels so different, man."

"So that's it? March 6th is the day they'll kill him?" Betty asks.

"Only if no last-minute appeal goes through," Pastor Prince says. "We can still hold out hope for a life-changing miracle though." He looks up at the big dark mahogany wood cross hanging nearby on the wall.

"We've got to check on Geno," I say, "I don't know how he's taking this news. His hopes were so high."

"Let's do it," he says.

§ § §

Pastor Prince is trying to keep Geno's spirits up as they reminisce and rap their first rhyme all over again, changing the lyrics slightly:

Road dog, boss hog

Keep that bond, flip that mon'

Christ love

Past death, brauh

When Geno realizes everything they say is being recorded, the two of them begin to speak more using their "rap" code words, a complex and secretive type of language that they must've made up as young boys turning into young men.

"We can teach you our secret language, but then we'd have to..." Pastor Prince cuts himself off short, each of us knowing what he planned to say.

It seems everything turns back to Geno's impending death date, no matter how much we try to avoid the topic, or put on happy, smiley faces that try to pretend everything is going to be okay.

Everything is most certainly not okay as far as Geno's life is concerned, and the more I've researched people who've been on death row for much longer, the more his situation starts to smack of unfair treatment.

It's almost as if by killing Geno, the state is hoping to finally put an end to the last traces of any rap-related violence hanging around the Left Coast, like California is floating the theory that since Dee is dead and Lasso is dead, Geno must now die in order to wrap the triangulation up into a neat and tidy bow of death. But Geno's death can't bring back the other two – and now that he recognizes his sins, his contrition means nothing to those who want to see him die. They want blood.

Part of it is the precedent-setting model this specific case provides: There's never been a mega-famous case like this whereby a popular young rapper kills his girlfriend, and is in turn then killed by her father, also a well-known rapper from his heyday and beyond.

The other cases of violence involving rappers in America either brought sensationalist headlines but no death – or no satisfying arrests made in the cases whereby a death did occur. The reason being the same mantra that Geno often repeated to me: No one wanted to pinpoint and report what they witnessed and then turn around to become victims themselves.

None of that mattered now. Geno's date of execution was approaching faster than any of us liked, and in between all our rallying, and performing hundreds of other acts that sought to get him a last-minute appeal, our group took to doing the one thing that mattered most to get him out of this predicament: We agreed to fast and pray.

§ § §

Candle-lit vigils are being held as people crowd outside the prison, giving San Quentin an eerie glow beyond the bay, as light can be seen for nearly a mile in each direction.

"This day seemed to come so soon," I lean over and whisper to Pastor Prince, feeling that high kind of feeling that fasting can bring, making one feel like they are not altogether there in the moment, but at the same time experiencing a great sense of power and closeness to heaven.

"I never thought this day would come *ever*," he replies, and for the first time I see past his pastor persona and am looking at a man who is steeling himself to say goodbye to his best friend.

From our research and experience, we know that these last 24 hours which could represent Geno's final day on this earth have been filled with a flurry of events in comparison to his everyday boring life in prison.

The warden already made special arrangements for certain friends and family members of Geno's to visit with him yesterday, and I felt privileged to be on that list – but no one could've felt more surprised than Pastor Prince and I when Geno's mother showed up.

"Thelma's here!" The whispers from those of us who'd been approved to be there the day prior – Geno's friends and other family members – were loud enough for the proud woman to hear as she strolled into the space, her lips pursed tightly, not saying a word.

"Mama," Geno said, nearly breaking down and falling torso-first into hers, calling for his mother in that raw and boyish way that many emergency personnel report that many dying men do – from the cockpits of plane recorders that catch audio recordings of professional pilots calling for their mothers, to the last disappearing breaths of 90-year-old perishing men who call for their moms even if they haven't seen them alive in years.

The room froze as Geno and his mother took a few minutes to simply stand close and take one another in, dropping all the pretenses of hate, non-forgiveness, stubbornness and false bravado fueling anger. There was no time for those type of "Who shot John?" nuances now.

At 6 o'clock on the night prior to his execution, prison officials had already placed Geno in the deathwatch location directly next to the place where they planned to execute him.

All I could think about though, was wanting to be there to see him enjoy his last meal from In-N-Out Burger that he requested, and watch him savor a lavish meal that didn't suck like prison fare.

Alas, the rules stated I couldn't come back until up to two hours before his scheduled execution, which means I was allowed to arrive in the witness room outside the lethal injection room around 10 p.m.

Now that I'm sitting here, twisting nervously in my seat and trying to play it off like I'm somewhere innocuous, as if anxiously waiting for a church service to begin – I look from the jade-colored bed in the lethal injection room, with its black straps that are waiting to hold Geno's limbs down as he's given a poisonous concoction, up to the clock above the bed.

I cannot wrap my mind around the fact that his life is set to expire in less than 120 minutes from now…

Chapter 8:

Life After Death

The area outside of San Quentin is alive and abuzz with media outlets from all over the world. White vans with all too familiar logos and names such as CNN, HLN, Fox News and even foreign ones have gathered in clusters, with the satellite transmission towers jetting tall towards the heavens out of the mobile communications trucks. Primarily online-based videographers from websites like TMZ have joined them, along with rogue citizen journalists and well known bloggers hovering their smartphones in the air to light up the night sky, or to illuminate their faces as they furiously text and live-blog the event at hand.

There are even helicopters circling over the prime real estate area that overlooks the northern parts of San Francisco Bay – not only for the news media to get a bird's eye view of the structure, but other helicopters are aloft for security reasons.

Geno's impending and planned death has caused a firestorm of outrage and elation all mixed into one glorious melting pot of turmoil on this night. "Pass Prop. 34!" read the signs held high by a cluster of organized folks who bounce their posters up and down as they shout the same chant that matches their signs and t-shirt sayings.

Another group stands by quietly, sipping coffee with "John 14:6" emblazoned on their shirts. More boisterous demonstrators have joined the peaceful protestors holding thin candles within cups that battle against the winds from San Pablo Bay.

Added to the melee are the rowdy folks who seem to be yelling for the media's sake alone, those simply trying to gain their 15 minutes of fame – as proven by the dot com names of their websites displayed promotionally on their hoodies – without a real depth of knowledge about the details of Geno's case.

"Free Geno Cide! Free Geno Cide!" they yell, shouting down those who try to get them to settle down and answer questions from news reporters.

As those protesting that Geno should be left alive come against those who want to see him put to death tonight grow louder and rowdier, the Richmond San Rafael Bridge region appears to be the battleground of a near riot. Battle gear dressed police stand at the ready, looking to their commander for the word to unleash the pepper spray, tear gas canisters and stun guns that each one has attached in holsters on their sides.

Thanks to Twitter, Facebook, Instagram, Pinterest and other social media websites, our "Save Geno" crew has put the spotlight on saving Geno's life, which has turned into a political rallying call against the death penalty, as well as an attempt at forgiveness for the revenge crime. In the near-decade since the last man was executed on these grounds, social media didn't even exist – and a blog was a word that drew blank stares or endless questions to clear up the confusion of everyone except those who knew about techie things like HTML and web logs.

Even those who miraculously had never heard of either rapper – and couldn't name a Geno Cide or Lasso hip hop song for the life of them – have weighed in on the issue, no doubt in large part due to what a hot button and heartfelt topic the death penalty represents.

It seems all the moderates have stayed home, most of them watching news coverage of the events streaming live on their mobile devices – or from the comfort of their living rooms. Those in the middle of the road regarding whether it's cruel and unusual punishment to shut down a healthy man's organs don't find it sufficient enough of a stance to warrant their driving down here to lend their opinions to the mix.

The extremists, on the other hand – those passionately consumed with upholding their rights as Americans to put to death people who've harmed others – are waving little electric chairs in the face of those who are nearly in tears with compassion over saving a life.

"DNA evidence has exonerated so many innocent people," one woman with long black and gray hair says with fervor into a broadcast camera lens as a reporter holds a microphone close to her mouth, and presses his hand against a small headphone transmission in his ear to hear direction from the nearby mobile control room.

"We can't be soft on crime," another man interjects, hijacking her interview. "If these killers didn't care about their victims, and they can rape and murder and torture people, we shouldn't coddle them. Hell, they're getting off the easy way by getting the injection shot. Better than what they gave their victims!"

"But that's not this case," the woman protests, and more people gather around behind the duo to begin shouting their opinions into the camera, until the reporter faces the camera himself and closes out the segment.

From within the prison, though, it is eerily quieter. Only the buzz of the choppers overhead and the low hum and rustling of voices give those inside the sense of the flurry of activity from beyond the walls.

We are pensive, with the gravity of the knowledge that a man's soul may very well transition from this earth to parts unknown within a short while.

§§§

"I'm really sorry y'all," Geno had hung his head and told all of us earlier – Pastor Prince, Kim, Swag, Betty, and I – as he met with us collectively during the 9 o'clock hour. The famous rapper had already been allowed to meet with at least six visitors individually during that time, and at the end, all of us as a group.

His mother Thelma had already chosen to receive her private conversation with her son, and not return back with the group to see him one last time. A stalwart to the end, Thelma's stubbornness and unwillingness to be seen as a weakling, or on level with our tight-knit group, seemed to have gotten the better of her once again. She reminded me of the old adage that "a leopard can't change its spots" in a walking, breathing version of hard-headedness.

Others of us, however, who've been around Geno the most this last year of life, soaked up every second that we were allowed to be in his presence.

"You know we're still praying for clemency, man," Pastor Prince had said, and adopted the tone of a hopeful boy at Christmas, having dropped the large and proud pastoral voice he normally reserved for women who'd recognize him in grocery stores or at the mall, and then interrupt his activities to ask for prayer.

Upon hearing that statement, Geno had given his old friend a look as if Pastor Prince were the one in trouble – as if with his gentle retort, he could have gotten him to face reality.

"All of the last-minute appeals have been lost, dude," Geno had told him, still seemingly trying to sound not as dire as the situation certainly called for. "Do you know what it would take for the governor to ring one of those phones?"

Without asking for further clarification, we'd all realized the last-minute reprieve phones of which Geno spoke – and our dulled mood belied the fact that supernaturally there was a unanimous understanding in the room that those would be the last few minutes we would all get to sit that close to Geno.

We simply knew he was ready to die. We could tell by his face, and the way it almost shone with another-worldliness that made him seem younger than his 45 years.

The awkward silence could not have been diverted by music or a sitcom to chase away the collective sad feelings, like during the times one may visit a downtrodden home with the hallmarks of chaos and tragedy – portraying the signs of alcoholism, abuse and neglect running rampant, all masked by a TV turned nearly as loud as it can go. Those times, it was as if blasting music or leaving *Good Times* blaring on an expensive flat screen HDTV mounted on the wall of a poverty-stricken home – where the elaborate electronic acted as the prize conquest and star trophy – would somehow transfer its miserable viewers into another, happier, funnier world vicariously.

Geno had spent enough of his childhood and formative years in that state of being, so he'd chosen to wile away the last hours that he was allowed to spend talking with us – and just lolling around, unanimated, as if we were Jewish folks sitting *shiva* even before the death happened – instead of watching television or listening to songs on the radio.

"It took me this long to realize that life is not all about me," Geno had said in the midst of the melancholy, huffing a little bit to himself. "Funny the things you begin to realize when you're really facing your own mortality, and not only talking about it or rapping about it in some fake song. You've been a good friend," Geno then turned and told Pastor Prince, echoing deep emotion held within those last five words.

"You too, Geno," he'd said, nearly unable to get the words out.

"Thank you for helping tell my story," Geno had said after looking at me. "I never could've imagined how some book could help me serve to leave a legacy on this land after I'm gone."

The weight of his statement pushed me to realize that the last chapter of Geno's life was indeed winding down, as could be felt like the thickness of a hot summer day in that room. I didn't want to take in his words, which to me would've meant we were all saying that this execution was okay, that it was somehow fair to hold this black man up as some kind of symbol of hate all across the USA based on past mistakes that he'd repented over and rap lyrics he'd recanted.

"It's not over. You can write another new song, making up for all the hate. It can't be over now," I'd said aloud, though my knee-jerk reaction was to hold back. But that would've been delaying the inevitable, I realized, and the potential last time you look into a man's eyes this side of heaven is not the time to start holding back, so I'd decided to say what was on my mind, rambling ranting emotions and all. "They should let you live – at least life without the possibility of parole. At least that much…"

"We can all accept this now," Geno had told our group, settling us down, as if we were the ones looking at the reality of a fatal dose of drugs soon to enter our bodies. "Save for some kind of miracle in the next couple of hours, this is going to happen. I will meet my Maker face to face," he'd said, and then had gazed upward in a way that let us all know this was a human being who knew beyond a doubt he'd soon be in a place a lot lovelier and closer to paradise than the dull room in which we all sat.

"Thank you for letting me tell your life story," I'd said, marveling at how the one preparing to be put to death was comforting those who'd live beyond him. "Thanks for trusting me with it."

"Keep it going," Geno had told me, and visions of epilogues and a series of books about the aftermath of his life flashed in my mind's eye, like words and quotations that danced around book pages and websites that I knew would make it to publication.

It was then that the gravity of his impending death washed over me. This wasn't a manufactured movie scene. That beige bank of phones with unlit red lights atop each one that rested on the wall inside the injection delivery room might not spring to life in the case of a last-minute stay of execution that spares Geno's life. Simply because we wanted Geno to remain alive and be set free in a whirlwind of activity from death row – and prison altogether, truthfully speaking – didn't mean that was how it was going to happen. Our minds may have replayed varying scenes whereby an under-the-wire call halted the executioner's needle hovering above Geno's IV in the same way that the Lord shouted "Stay your hand, Abraham!" as he prepared to plunge a knife into his so-called "only begotten" son Isaac, but our guts told us another outcome awaited.

Keep it going, he'd said, and that reminded me of the updated endings to books about him that he wouldn't see, articles I couldn't print out and send to him, or read over collect-call conversations interspersed with that annoying announcement. Conflicting waves of relief over the miles I'd no longer have to drive and the prison-wearying routine we'd all endured just to see him swirled with the grief that a man we'd grown to love would be no more.

He existed.

That was what people should know about Geno Stone. He existed – and yes, he did wrong, but he also changed his way of thinking in the end. At least he changed at all, unlike those who stubbornly keep up the same façade after it's too late to change a thing, like that rich man who begged Abraham to send Lazarus to dip his finger in water to cool the tongue of the man being tortured and in agony in the depths of hell. But it was too late, for a "chasm fixed" couldn't be traversed.

Geno is not that man, nor was he several minutes ago, as he made the rounds, seemingly making amends and the circular journey of a personal connection with every one of us present.

"And you," Geno had pointed to Swag, "keep rapping. Keep spitting, girl. You've got that mad flow."

"Man, dog, for you to tell me that," she'd replied, letting go of her hardened persona for the moment. "That means so much to me. You don't even know. I'm going to write a song in your honor."

"Do that," he'd confirmed. "Do that then. You helped me look at women in a different way – and I got mad respect for you, for real – on the real tip."

"Word," she'd said, falling into that common street vernacular that served when other words failed. "Real talk."

Swag shook her head and we all offered closed-mouthed, slightly upturned mouth motions that attempted to force themselves into smiles, like when folks attend a funeral and are happy to see long-lost relatives, but don't want to portray too much happiness in the face of a solemn situation.

"Thank you all for fighting for me so hard," Geno had said, rapidly, as he saw a guard approaching to escort him away. "Don't blame yourselves. This was completely *my fault*. You all did the best you could. My life is meant to end now."

"We love you!" I'd blurted out of nowhere, embarrassed of myself, that is, until the gang unleashed their own bundle of raw love and emotions, too.

"Yeah, man, I really love you," Pastor Prince said just as quickly. "Remember to be absent from the body is to be present with the Lord."

"I'm ready to see Him, man," Geno had smiled in return and as an afterthought, had added in a rapping cadence, "*Christ's love, past death, brauh,*" that brought an impromptu side-mouth twisted smile out of the man of God, too.

"Lucas was my son," Betty had said slowly, "but I consider you my son as well, Geno. You can rest easy in knowing that God our Lord has forgiven you for the acts you've committed – because you've admitted them and repented."

"That means the world to me," he'd said.

Kim was the sole one from the group who had tried to speak, to say some significant and long-lasting words to the man she'd known since her teen years – who'd been through the elation of birthing his child and the deepest pains and lows of losing that same daughter to a violent death, but she could not say one word. It had seemed like 20 years of happiness, hurt, pain, loss and love had ended up caught right there in her closed voice box, her larynx shut from a well of emotion rising up from her chest.

"Baby, I know," Geno had told her, their eyes meeting, heads shaking in tandem. "I know, don't cry. It's all right."

With that, Geno nodded, and several guards approached to take him away to be held in the holding cell for condemned prisoners like him as they awaited execution.

§ § §

"There are certain specific grieving emotions or psychological effects you may experience after watching an execution," a woman is advising a small select group of media participants who are preparing to enter a different witness viewing room from ours.

"Consider these warnings prior to partaking in the witnessing of this death," she continues. "Other people have reported not being able to stop thinking about the death afterward – or of having dreams and nightmares about the event continually after it has occurred. One particular witness reported that his father kept recalling an execution he'd watched many years ago, a memory that continued to come back to him frequently the weeks prior to his own death. We only tell you these things to prepare you."

Of the three rooms – all of which are lit very brightly, like that of a stark white operating room – Pastor Prince, Swag, Kim, Betty and I will enter the compact room on the north side of the space. This is not the room reserved for media personnel who've made the cut and get to chronicle the events from the inside or for biographers. This is the viewing room set aside for Geno's family and friends. I feel honored and humbled.

All of the rooms have large windows that give us an unobstructed view to the bright green gurney that everyone looks at briefly and then away from again – an empty bright-green dentist chair whose black straps designed to hold a prisoner down flat on his back now hang freely. The chair is an imposing sight in the middle of the room, and there is plenty of room around the showpiece for several bodies to move about. Restraints for legs dangle from the lime-colored injection table where Geno – now known as "the condemned prisoner" – is scheduled for execution.

Clemency from the governor of the state of California was Geno's last hope. But clemency has been denied. The five of us shift quietly in our own individual chairs as none of us offers words to Thelma, who sits in stony silence, staring straight ahead at the empty death chamber.

"It's time," Pastor Prince whispers, nudging me with his elbow and nodding toward the execution chamber as Geno is escorted inside by seemingly more guards that necessary.

"There must be 20 people in there!" I whisper back.

"Maybe because it's a special case," Swag says.

Geno has been chained around his waist, and that chain is attached to a set of handcuffs. The whole getup makes him walk with a weirdly exaggerated, shuffling kind of gait. I notice he is now wearing a brand new pair of denim pants and a blue work shirt, one of the many things that strikes me as ironic in this moment before death, like when a comedian once asked if they swab a prisoner's arms with alcohol prior to giving the lethal injection, and if so, why? None of these things are laughable during this moment, only curious observations about a surreal experience that come rushing back to my mind in snatches for some reason.

Geno doesn't fight at all as he is escorted into the death chamber right next to our room, several minutes prior to his scheduled pre-midnight death time. Next, the guards place him on the gurney and prepare to secure his body to the reclined chair. We can tell this is done with the precise orderliness of guards who are following a specific set of prison and state rules – even if execution is something rarely performed.

"There will be no crying fits or hysterical screaming or outbursts allowed during the execution process," we'd been warned by a prison official prior to entering this room, so many of us are keeping our emotions in check so we'll be allowed to stay until the end.

"And no demonstrations of any kinds will be tolerated during the procedure," we'd learned. I found that quite ironic, considering the numerous amounts of protests going on outside the prison.

Our viewing room participants are stock still as Geno's ankles are first fastened securely to the table, and next the prison officials move up slightly to strap down his knees. Geno stares straight up at the ceiling and waits motionless as another set of executioners next secure each of his arms. Finally, they pull a long strap across his waist and then place a shoulder harness around him, which holds him down even more.

Geno appears somewhat serene, and I have a flashback to one of his old videos from back in the day, when he strutted freely and peacock-proud from one end of the crowded stage to the next. He didn't need BWO or any of the multitudinous hype men he'd had on stage back then – he could command a room with his persona and voice. And yet here he is once more, commanding a crowd and surrounded by people, but for a very different reason and result.

Only after they've tested and tugged on all the straps to ensure their stability do they then remove the cuffs and chains from Geno's wrists and waist. That's when I begin to understand that the people carrying out this death sentence are risking their lives, too, and my mind flashes to a movie-like scene where the inmate breaks free through a wayward strap and uses the same injection needle planned for him to kill a guard instead.

But this isn't the newest release at the movie theaters, or one of Geno's videos from back in the day – wherein he cast himself in similar death-defying roles like Jesus hanging on a cross – but we are witnesses to a real-life scene in front of our eyes that can't be turned off or recast or rewound, like so many films saved to our DVR machines back at home.

Geno is being outfitted with a heart monitor whose cable cords run the length of a small space over to a machine, one that is attached to a printer that provides vital information to a different prison worker whose job it is to study it carefully.

Before long, Geno's body language turns from calm to nervous as he twitches and jerks even from within the restraints. His breathing appears shallow as his chest starts rising up and down rapidly.

I can still hear the helicopters faintly rumbling overhead in the distance as one guard taps another, and a man steps forward to view no gallery in particular as he opens a folded 8 ½ by 11 sheet of paper and begins to read methodically from the printout.

"Geno Stone has been found guilty of first degree murder," he states succinctly. "And as such, we will now proceed with the execution as ordered by the court, after the condemned gives his final statement."

One of the executing guards holds a wireless microphone to Geno's lips, and he tilts his head slightly upward to get close to the device, so that his broadcasted last words can be heard clearly throughout the rooms. A hush befalls our small space, even though it was already relatively silent. It's like we are all holding our breath, too, so that the inhalation and exhalation of air won't interfere with what Geno will say.

He is a man familiar with a microphone, but not like this – one so small that's being held by another to Geno's mouth. As he naturally clears his throat, the sound Geno makes is reminiscent of so many intros to an untold number of his rap songs, all those lyrically lascivious poems that many times began with his macho grunt and the standard, "Yo!" before launching into a diatribe about some easy woman or fast money or faster car.

This last statement – his last performance, as it were, is miles apart from the stadiums he filled all around the world. These final words aren't being rhymed across a "dope beat" or draped in the braggadocio that made men want to be just like him, and at least for the women who weren't afraid of him, to be with him – no questions asked, no niceties needed before going to bed with the rapping superstar. No, these words are from the heart of a truly repentant man, one who isn't going to his grave full of pride and calling himself the captain of his own soul or master of his own fate.

When he begins to speak, his voice starts out in a strained whimper, softer and removed of the type of put-on manliness that men usually reserve for one another, switching tones from soft pillow talk with their wives when their fathers or male friends call.

"I'm so sorry to everyone I hurt," Geno says, straining upward to allow his voice to be heard clearly.

"May God forgive me for what I've done, for taking out my anger on Lucas and ending his life unnecessarily. I forgive him for what he did to Dee – and hope he is in the better place where I'm going. Forgive me, Kim, for the way I treated you and neglected our daughter. I pray I soon meet our sweet baby girl in heaven with Jesus."

Kim quietly weeps into her palms as the guard pauses for any more words from Geno – and when he sees there are no more forthcoming, he takes the microphone away and turns off the switch that broadcasts sounds into the accompanying rooms.

Next, several executioners work in conjunction to tape Geno's hands, wrists and fingers until they resemble those of a mummy's covered extremities. A few of the men swing the table that holds his body around and wait, giving Geno one more time to lift his head up and look around at his strapped-down frame and to those watching him.

Geno mouths the words "I love you" to his mom. In turn, Thelma holds up her thumb, index finger and pinkie finger of her right hand and makes a swooping motion toward her son.

"That means 'I love you' in sign language," I whisper extremely quietly to no one in particular, too quiet for anyone else to hear my thoughts but myself.

Geno sees her motion, then drops his head back helplessly onto the chair as a woman inserts an IV into his arm in two different spots, using two different veins, just in case one breaks or gets blocked. A regular saline solution begins to flow through the IV.

The clock above his head reads 11:55 p.m. inside this new $853,000 lethal injection facility at San Quentin, the selfsame one whereby another condemned man waited for quite some time for the IV to be successfully injected into his arm. There have been no such troubles this time with Geno.

His veins were readily apparent and easily found, primed to be used as the vehicle to put him to death by the new single drug injection – the first Californian to experience the process.

As the drug is injected into Geno's IV line, he soon after gives three snorts, as if snoring in puffing breaths. Then, pretty anti-climactically, he looks as if he simply falls asleep. I imagine the violence he might be feeling inside, though, and try to push away scenes that stick with me from *Dead Man Walking* from years prior – a movie so intense that when it ended, the bulk of the downtown Chicago audience refused to get up and file out like normal, but sat in an intelligent stupor to talk about the film.

The scenes that come rushing to my memory are the ones whereby the characters described that although the lethal injection process can look peaceful, there could be a whole bunch of painful things going on inside of the person being put to death, like a patient who becomes paralyzed by anesthesia during an operation – but can't call out to the operating team to tell them that they can still feel every cut and each suture, that their nerves are still alive.

As expected, with Geno there is no wild twitching or thrashing beneath the straps. It is over within minutes, if not seconds. One of the many people in the execution chamber steps forward tentatively to obtain his heart rate information, and, finding no signs of life, he nods to another man, who steps forward and speaks to the witnessing rooms.

"Geno Stone has been confirmed dead, put to death by lethal injection at 11:59 p.m.," he states firmly, projecting his voice like a palace guard.

While there are signs of unseen life moving about the media witness room – with reporters no doubt rushing around to live blog the death time, their observances and to leak any illegal photos they were able to snag during the event – our room just sits there, looking at the lifeless body of Geno Stone.

We are unable to move for a long time.

§ § §

At home within hours, I cannot sleep. The day and night has been a whirlwind of so many people and such high emotions, coupled with a disappointing denouement. It's too hard to wrap my head around the face that Geno is no more – that the birth date on his life's timeline now has a death date bookmarking the other end.

I didn't want it to end like this, I think to myself, and glance to my left at the rendering of a painting of Jesus. Deeper still, I feel that somehow it's okay that it has ended this way.

"Rest in sweet sleep," I whisper aloud.

§ § §

"You know I saw Geno last night," Pastor Prince tells me matter-of-factly, hesitantly, the way that you tell someone something that you've got to get out of your belly and off of your psyche, but you don't know how they'll take it. "He came to me, like at the front of my home."

It's been one week since Geno died, and yet it is all we can ever talk about, like two hurting people trying to console one another. Losing Geno was akin to losing a major tooth or rib or organ – all the remaining teeth and ribs and organs draw closer or function differently in its absence, as if to try and make up for the crushing loss.

We are inside the offshoot church location, moving in a slow motion type of pace as we tidy up.

"You did?" I ask, pausing from packing up the "Save Geno" regalia into boxes at the conference room that's served as command central for quite a few months now.

"Yeah," he explains, eager now that I haven't looked at him like he's crazy, but in an accepting manner. "I was walking out the front door with my kids to just let off some steam and play outside in the rain, and right when I opened the storm door, I saw a reflection of Geno's face right there through the tempered plastic."

"I've seen visions like that before," I admit, and Pastor Prince and I can both see ourselves growing more excited and yet relaxed at the same time, like having found a long lost family member who doesn't think you're strange for believing in a spiritual world beyond the vision of most people.

"You have?"

"Yes – I've seen quite a few things beyond this world. But tell me about Geno," I urge.

"It was very brief – only for a quick second – and I know it wasn't the reflection of our TV in the living room or anything, because my kids had turned off the television, so there were no images of any people on the screen," he says. "I couldn't even see anything beyond his face. I didn't see his clothes or body or anything, only a flash of his face – but it was so awesome."

"I get it. Man, I'm glad he came to you and not me," I say. "I prayed he wouldn't. Did he say anything?"

"No, but it was like he was almost coming to play outside with us, like when we were younger." Pastor Prince begins smiling at a memory, in spite of his saddened state. "Sometimes when his mom would be tripping too hard, he'd show up at my door – and he wouldn't even have to say a word about anything. We'd just hang out, you know?"

"Yes," I nod. "I believe you. I've had more than one person tell me how someone who they loved who'd recently died visited them. But other than that, I've seen visions of God's angels or Jesus – and of a little girl's face. The year my dad died, I even saw a black and white eye in the rays of sun lingering over his house. I took it as a good sign from above, like protection or a good message."

"I think it really was," he says. "I don't think it was anything evil. And even though Geno didn't say anything, in my spirit I felt like he was saying he wanted to have fun and hang out with the crew once more before departing this earth for good."

Pastor Prince and I look down at all the "Save Geno" remnants of bumper stickers and T-shirts remaining, and around at the conference room. Suddenly, loud voices – distinctly female – can be heard coming from the hall.

We are startled, but before long, Kim, Swag and Betty all enter the room, carrying boxes and bags.

"Hey y'all," Swag says, heaving her oversized cardboard box onto the conference room table. "We got the stuff."

"What stuff?" Pastor Prince asks.

"What Geno wanted," Kim says, and with that and a bit of flourish, she flips open a t-shirt from the box that reads "Our Kids Keepers" on its front. She holds it close to her body and hugs the shirt.

"You all don't mess around, do you?" I ask.

"We can't give up the cause," Betty says as she begins to unpack another, smaller box with stationery and pens that read "Our Kids Keepers" on them as well.

"We did promise Geno," Pastor Prince says, looking around the space. "So – same room, new mission, huh?"

The trio of women all nod in unison, so Pastor Prince and I begin nodding as well. The last traces of the "Save Geno" memorabilia have been packed away as we all begin unpacking the "Our Kids Keepers" signs, clothing and accouterments to put them in their place.

§ § §

"What do you think about this one? Does this look legit?" Swag asks, showing her iPad tablet to a group of us as we eat lunch inside a spic-and-span clean In-N-Out Burger joint that offers a view of the bustling Dwight D. Eisenhower Highway in Fairfield, California, and the rising lands beyond.

"Let me see," Pastor Prince says, taking the device from her hands to read it up close. "You know I can spot a fake or a scammer from a mile away."

"What's it about?" Kim asks, dipping a French fry in ketchup.

"This girl sent us an email saying she needs $10,000 to get a new apartment to get away from her abusive boyfriend," Swag says. "I'm trying to figure out if she's for real or not."

"Who is she?" Betty asks, leaning over and squinting, trying to read the email over Pastor Prince's shoulders. "Did she give us her name?"

Before Swag can answer, sudden yelling shatters the peacefully calm restaurant. A young pretty teenager and a tall man wearing a white and red tracksuit are the source of the commotion, right near the counter at the cash register.

The cashier looks puzzled as the man looks from the woman he is standing next to over to a different guy and back again, but he continues to order his food – special items off the secret menu – as if using it for a cover to mask and consider his next move.

"Are you kidding me?" he explodes, enraged, turning his attention back to his girlfriend as if he's no longer able to continue the charade. "You're looking at this guy over here? You're always screwing everybody!"

"What are you talking about? I wasn't looking at anybody! And even if I was – so you're the only one who gets to mess around, huh?" she taunts. "It's not right when I do it, huh Byron?"

The man presses his hands to his face and stomps toward the door. "I'll show you what's right when I leave your butt here."

"Byron!" she screams. "You're not leaving me here."

"Watch me," he says, still walking. "Have that clown take you home. Probably some weak punk anyway."

The teen girl turns and dramatically runs after him, grabbing onto his jacket, pulling on his pants, and any piece of fabric she can grasp. "You better not leave me here. This is foul."

"Get off me," Byron shouts, flicking her away from him to the point where she stumbles against the large garbage container bolted to the floor.

"*Ow*," she whines and moans, but he keeps charging out the door. She tries to charge out after him, but Pastor Prince bolts up and stops her.

"Let him go, honey," he says, putting both arms on her shoulders to steady her and get her attention. "We can all get you a ride home. Just let him cool off."

She looks a little leery in the direction of the stranger holding her, so all of us women get up and approach her to let her know we are in a group together.

"Don't worry, honey," Betty chimes in, touching her shoulder. "You'll be safer if you stay here."

"What's your name, sweetie?" I ask. "Just calm down and tell us your name. It's okay."

She breathes an exasperated sigh and looks down. "Sylvia."

Her tone sounds as if there's a twinge of a Spanish accent to her name, the way she pronounces it.

"Okay, Sylvia," Pastor Prince says calmly, all the while keeping an eye on Byron, who is walking around his gigantic, stark white Escalade with gold-colored, spinning rims in the parking lot, closing and opening various doors. As he does, loud and violent rap music filters out, growing louder each time he opens a door, then more muted when he closes it. I can't help but shake my head a bit when I hear the decidedly distinct lyrics of one of Lasso's most popular songs.

"Can you tell us if your boyfriend has any guns in that SUV?" Betty asks, just as sweetly and calmly as if she'd asked her for a chicken potpie recipe.

"No – not on him," Sylvia says.

"Does he have any at home?" Pastor Prince says.

She nods. "A few. A butterfly knife and some nunchuks. Plus one more knife – you know the kind, with those serrated edges?"

"Yeah, I know. My ex-husband used to have the same kinds of weapons," I say. "Just stay right in here for a minute and let's let the situation calm down and diffuse before you do anything."

Byron gets back in the driver's seat of his SUV, waiting as the engine idles and the muted hip-hop music thumps from inside. He glares toward Sylvia, as if he's actually waiting for her to return to the vehicle – but after a full minute or two, he throws the SUV in reverse and screeches out of the lot with fast and furious driving maneuvers.

Sylvia lets out a whimper. "See...I knew he was gonna leave me. He ain't right."

Kim puts her arm around the young teen. "It's okay, honey. We can take you wherever you need to be, let's talk first...all right...and make sure you're safe. Okay?"

Sylvia pulls out her cell phone and scrolls through it, looking from this odd bunch of people in front of her back to the phone again. "Okay," she says.

§ § §

"What'd y'all call this?" Sylvia says, looking around the conference room, slightly calmer than before. She has stopped shaking from the prior melee at the burger joint.

"We call it 'Our Kids Keepers,'" Pastor Prince answers.

"Who's Dee?" she asks, still giving our group the side-eye as she walks around the table, picking up and putting down various brochures that explain the foundation.

"You remember Geno Stone?" I ask. "Geno Cide – the rapper?"

Sylvia turns animated. "Yeah, girl. That was my dude. But Lasso was the *shiz-nizzle* for real though. All of that mess was such a tragedy. What a loss."

"Well, Dee was Geno's daughter," Kim says. "Our daughter."

Sylvia opens the tri-fold brochure in her hand and spots a photo of Dee. She looks from Kim to Dee and around the room once more.

"Oh, snap! You were Dee's mom? Oh my goodness – it's so nice to meet you," she says, overly excited before catching herself. "I mean, I'm so sorry for your loss."

"It's okay," Kim says. "You kind of remind me of her, you know. The way you talk, the things you say."

"Oh yeah?" Sylvia says, her side-eye glances returning. "So...why'd y'all bring me here?"

"Sylvia, I'm Lasso's mom," Betty says, sticking out her hand towards the girl. "Betty Bridgeport."

"Woooowwwww…" she says in return, shaking her head slowly. "I can't believe this."

"The only reason we have this foundation – this 'Our Kids Keepers' – is because my son killed his girlfriend," Betty explains gently, "and in return, Geno killed him for it in revenge."

"I saw it all on the news," Sylvia says, her mouth ajar in disbelief.

"So then you must've seen Geno's recent execution, too," Pastor Prince says.

"Yep. Fools was blowing up Twitter over that mess," she answers.

"Well, none of us wanted Geno's death to be in vain – not even Geno," he continues. "So he had us start this mission to help girls who we think may be in trouble."

"What kind of trouble?" she asks, averting all of our eyes as she slides an index finger across the conference room table, drawing invisible swerves with her digit.

"You know," I say, "it could be anything. I mean, I remember when I was a teenager I got into all sorts of mess – unplanned pregnancies, drug use. And then I ended up hooking up with an abusive boyfriend…"

Sylvia keeps looking down, a stance that allows tears to begin seeping down from her eyes. After a bit of awkward silence, she speaks again.

"So, how many girls have y'all helped so far with this mission?" she asks.

"You'll be the first one," Pastor Prince says.

With that, she looks up – with a sense of relief gracing her face.